DESTROYER OF PLANETS

NEON OCTOPUS OVERLORD SERIES BOOK ONE

LA JOHNSON

CHEMICAL ZOMBIE PRESS

This book is a work of fiction. The names, characters and events in this book are the products of the author's imagination or are used fictitiously. Any similarity to real persons living or dead is coincidental and not intended by the author.

Published by Chemical Zombie Press LLC

Cover Artwork by Venkatesh Sekar
Editing by Kerry J. Donovan

For Mom & Dad

Chapter 1

Drexyl woke the same way he had since the start of his captivity—with a tentacle wrapped around his ankle and in a fit of high pitched screaming.

"I'm awake. Stars. Why don't you just kill me already and get it over with?" he muttered.

The Neon Blue Octopus Overlord slithered closer.

"Boundaries, you," Drexyl said, "we've talked about this."

"Yes," the Overlord hissed as she squirmed closer, "we have."

Living in the cushy lair of the Octopus Overlord wasn't all it was cracked up to be. She was known by different titles such as Overseer of the galaxy, Neon Octopus Overlord, and officially as the appointed Most Efficient Being in the galaxy.

“Stop it, you.” Drexyl held up a hand against her advance. She had a name of course. Everything had a name. Drexyl just couldn't pronounce it. And now, thanks to a gambling debt the size of a small planet's GDP, he was in bondage to her, forever. As usual, he hoped to make it past breakfast.

"Tut, tut," she said in her echoing metallic voice. "How many times have I asked you to call me by name? Ttszooodjdeaaaarrr. How hard is that?"

Actually, it was really hard. Between the metallic echo of her voice and her thick otherworld accent, Drexyl could never quite make out the exact pronunciation.

"Fine," he said, "I'll call you Soda." It was awkward calling her "you" all the time, and he didn't want to offend her, so he picked something easy and decided to go with it. He watched her physical reaction, which was not immediately homicidal. He exhaled in relief.

"Soda. Hmmm, I shall consider this name." The creature drew even closer, and Drexyl was enveloped in neon blue tentacles. He cringed and emitted a small scream. In the center of all the tentacles, her head was oval, and altogether too big for the neck that came with it.

Drexyl shuddered. He tried to reach his happy place—a hammock on the beach with a breeze. His happy place was getting harder and harder to reach.

This was not at all how he expected his life to play out. Yet here he was, living with a neon alien octopus who was constantly threatening to asphyxiate him. What were the odds?

Anyway, Drexyl had decided that he was going to do whatever was necessary until he could figure a way out of his situation. He didn't want to die. He was too attractive, for one thing. And fun. There was that time at that party where he had done that thing that made everybody laugh. He couldn't remember what it was, but he remembered the look on everyone's face. And their howls of laughter.

A few minutes later, Soda withdrew and slithered away to sit on her throne in front of the television.

Drexyl followed her and slumped into a nearby chair to watch television with her, there being a distinct lack of anything else to do. On the plus side, she had a giant, flat, high definition screen. On the minus side, her taste in shows sucked.

Drexyl, after thinking about it, was proud of the nickname he'd given her. Soda. Thankfully, she seemed okay with it. The whole living arrangement was awkward enough without tripping over names.

"You know," he said during a commercial break, "for somebody who's in charge of the entire galaxy, you have an awful lot of free time."

This caused what Drexyl guessed was amused sputtering on her part. "I am the most powerful being in the galaxy," she cooed. "In fact, I'm immortal. Why not enjoy my time? For instance, this pitiful galaxy's leaders are always inviting me to go to their stupid, boring meetings. They try to demand reports and input and answers, but it's tedious," she wheezed at him through rubbery lips. "I don't do the things that other beings consider important because I don't have to. That's the meaning of real power."

She sighed and ran a sucker-encrusted tentacle across his face. He gritted his teeth.

"Immortality's a funny thing, Drexyl. What nobody tells you is that after millennia to reflect, you realize there are far worse things in the universe than death. Endless monotony. Finding out your favorite restaurant has gone out of business. Budget meetings."

Drexyl wondered what she was going on about. He scooted backward, away from the wobbly head, but the tentacles were always with him. The ooze sloughing off them made his ankles itch.

Suddenly, the picture on the television screen turned fuzzy and pixilated.

Soda must have seen the change out of the corner of her eye. She turned her attention back to the television and whacked it with a tentacle.

"Remind me to call the stupid cable company," she told him. Whack. "I'm only the Supreme Overseer of the whole galaxy." Whack. "Just how important do you have to be to get a signal around here?"

The picture reappeared in crystal sharp focus.

"At least the commercial is still on," Drexyl said, "you didn't miss anything." A blur of neon movement caught his eye. "Hey, are you alright?"

Soda had jumped off of her throne and backed up. Her eyes bulged, and she pointed at the screen. "Did you see that? The message on the screen? The one that popped up when the commercial disappeared?"

Drexyl shook his head. "I only saw static. There was a message? Was it from the cable company?"

She grabbed an old coffee cup and threw it against the wall. It crashed noisily into a thousand pieces.

Drexyl jumped up and retreated across the room.

Soda scratched the side of her head with a tentacle and started pacing back and forth, carefully avoiding the shattered pieces of coffee cup on the floor.

This was the most upset Drexyl had seen her in his two years of captivity. He guessed it probably was the cable company. It usually had this effect on people.

"What did the message say?" Drexyl asked. "Did it tell you to restart your cable box? That's what my messages always say."

"No. It didn't tell me to restart the cable box." She squinted her bulging eyes at him. "Are you familiar with the word Thaaraa?"

He thought about it and shook his head. "No."

"It's a message in an ancient language. And it's not good news."

"Is something wrong with our cable service?"

Soda turned to him and raged. "It has nothing to do with the blasted cable company! What it means is that I've got to move up the end of the Celestial program. Do you have any idea how long it took me to kidnap and train all those Celestials?" Her whole body slumped. "It means I'm running out of time to cover my tracks."

* * *

KIRIAN BLINKED. She was standing over a screaming guy in an expensive suit. She had her favorite curved blade in her hand. That explained the screaming. The two of them were in a cubicle. She had no idea how or when she had got here. Also, her watch alarm was going off. She hit snooze. It seemed like the best option since she couldn't remember why it was beeping in the first place.

"Who are you?" she asked him. "And what am I doing here?" Her mind raced. She couldn't remember anything. Not entering the office, not pulling out the weapon, nothing. She re-sheathed her sword.

The cubicle dweller stopped screaming and blinked at her, watching her put away her weapon. He hyperventilated for a moment and then appeared to recover slightly.

"I-I'm Carl. You came in here waving that sword. A-And apparently, you're stealing my signed photo of the Star Slug." He pointed at the photo in her hand. Kirian looked down at the shiny, signed photo and slumped her shoulders.

"Nice," she told him, glancing at it for a moment. She tossed it on his desk.

"I bought it at Galaxy Con last month," he replied. "Cost me a fortune."

"I'll bet. Sorry about that. I haven't been myself lately." She ran her fingers through her dark hair, wondering what to do next. She glanced at her watch. In fact, she couldn't remember anything from the previous half hour or so.

Kirian was confused. *When did I start blacking out and plundering locals? I'm a brawler, but I've never been a thief.*

The man sat up and looked at her. In fact, he was staring. "Hey," he said, "you're Kiriell, Wrecker of Worlds, the legendary Celestial, right?"

She knelt next to him, smiling in an attempt to put him at

ease. "Actually, it's Kirian, Destroyer of Planets. Thank you so much for noticing. You've been spending quality time on the dark net, haven't you?" She raised an eyebrow at him.

Kirian had spent time fostering a fun alter ego of herself on the dark net. One of the only perks of working involuntarily in Celestial for the Octopus Overlord in charge of the galaxy was getting to choose your own title. She decided to be Kirian, Destroyer of Planets and have fun with it. Life in captivity could be boring.

"You get that the whole Planet Destroying thing is ironic, right?" she asked.

"Er, I guess so."

Her watch alarm buzzed again. "But seriously, your planet is about to be deleted. I'm very sorry; it's not my decision. Apparently, I'm just a lackey running around doing as I'm told until I lose my mind and start unconsciously robbing people."

She sighed. Then she showed him her bracelets. "I have no choice. I'm a prisoner of the Octopus Overlord."

"The Most Efficient Being in the Galaxy?"

"That's the one. Yeah."

"Why would she delete my planet?"

"No idea," said Kirian, standing. "Good luck. I gotta go, there's somebody I still have to kill."

Chapter 2

Ari rounded the corner and stopped outside the door of her boss's office. Her heart was pounding. She clutched a stack of paperwork in her hand.

As nervous as she was, she had never been more certain about anything in her life. The numbers her boss had given her were wrong, immeasurably wrong.

It wasn't just the numbers, either, there was something more to it. Something she couldn't quite put her finger on. This was one of several hundred daily moments that she wished she had taken the job on Horath instead.

A level-three intelligence like herself was obviously wasted on this planet and this company. And furthermore, the boss, Mr. Brake, had been blocking her transfer requests for over a year.

Ari steeled herself, took a deep breath and threw the door open without knocking.

Mr. Brake looked up from his desk and rolled his eyes at her. "What is it now, Ari?"

"These numbers," Ari said, "they don't add up the way you said they would." Ari shook the papers at him.

Both the terror of the situation and the excitement of finally standing up to him combined to pump adrenaline through her system. Ari gulped down more oxygen.

"You're paid to crunch the numbers," he said coolly, "not to think."

Ari's cheeks got hot. She gritted her teeth into a forced smile. "What I think is that you cut every corner imaginable, and now we are the subject of several lawsuits."

His face tightened. "And that's what we pay the lawyers for."

"Then there's the matter of the several million Galactic Credits in missing funds." Ari blurted it out and then froze for a moment. She knew that she'd crossed a line, and that there was no going back. Somewhere in the back of her mind, she started working on her CV.

Her boss stood, sizing her up as if seeing her for the first time. A vein on his forehead pulsed to imaginary electronica music. "You have no idea what you're talking about," he said in barely measured tones.

"On the contrary, I have all the proof right here." She waved the papers at him again. What part of this was he not getting?

Mr. Brake sat back down at his desk, grabbed his phone and dialed. "That does it. You're fired. Security," he bellowed, "I need you on the thirteenth floor. A very recently fired employee just assaulted me. Call the police as well, would you?"

"Assaulted?" Ari screamed. "You lying pig!" A finger tapped her shoulder from behind. Ari couldn't turn around though, because she couldn't risk breaking eye contact with the lying son of a wormhole since she was stuck in some sort of primal bureaucratic standoff. And losing.

"I'm a little busy," said Ari, not turning around. "You'll just have to wait your turn."

Ari was tingling with horror at the recent developments. It didn't feel real. Did he really just contact security and police? He was the real criminal here.

She sucked in a breath. The situation was spiraling out of

control and was now well past her worst nightmare. The room started to spin. *Get a grip, Ari.*

Another tap on her shoulder brought a sense of relief. At least there was a witness to the non-assault. "Hang on," Ari said, turning to face the shoulder-tapper and holding up an index finger.

Behind her stood an athletic looking girl with long dark hair and a curved sword.

Ari took a step back from the armed girl. How fast is security in this building? The sword felt like overkill in this particular situation. Was she going to jail before all of this got sorted out? Would her entire career be ruined by this idiot? She decided to try to convince Sword Girl to arrest him instead.

“Look, you were here when he said I assaulted him. You tapped me on the shoulder, remember? You're a witness that he lied. Arrest him, not me.”

Ari searched Sword Girl's face for signs she was getting through to her. Sword Girl looked conflicted. No, disinterested. Maybe even a strange combination of the two. Ari pressed on. “These papers, I have proof that this man is a criminal.”

"Enjoy jail." Mr. Brake smirked when she made no move to arrest him.

Ari looked to Mr. Brake, then back to Sword Girl, who now had a gun pointed at Ari's head.

Ari threw her hands in the air wondering where the gun had come from. “Hey, if you're security, then where's your uniform?” Sword Girl was wearing jeans and a hoodie. Under normal circumstances, Ari would have caught on sooner. She bit her lip.

Sword-Girl stepped forward and waved the gun from Ari to Mr. Brake and then back again, unable to make up her mind.

Then she pointed it back at Mr. Brake and fired. He slumped over his desk.

Ari gasped. "Who are you?"

"I'm not security, Ari," she said.

"I figured that out. How do you know my name?"

Sword Girl blinked at her. She was taller than Ari, and her long dark hair had luminescent tips. Ari would have been fascinated if she weren't so terrified.

"Look, I know your name because I studied you to kill you," she said, stashing the sword inside her hoodie. "It's my job. Long story. I have an evil boss too." She tilted her head in Mr. Brake's direction. "I'll fill you in some time. Anyway, I've changed my mind about killing you, but it's a limited time offer."

"If you're not security, then why did you do that to Mr. Brake?"

"What do you care? He's a jerk. And besides, he's fine." Swordgirl showed the ray gun proudly to Ari. "This gun is nothing more than experimental sleep-ray technology. Very fun. And it slays at parties."

"Parties?" Ari asked. "What are you talking about?"

"Well, this planet is pretty uptight. So probably not at these parties, but at other parties on fun planets, it slays, trust me."

Ari had no idea what to say to that.

"Ari, we have to go. This planet is about to be deleted."

Deleted? What was she talking about? Who could delete an entire planet?

"Look," she said, "I'm Kirian, Destroyer of Planets." She said it as if that would clear everything up. It didn't. "Your planet is going to be deleted. Soon."

She raised an eyebrow and pointed at her watch. "I was sent to kill you, remember? But according to your profile, you're a level-two intelligence, and I need your help. So, I need you to come with me."

Ari was fully prepared to ask follow-up questions about Kirian's title, but those were washed away by the level-two intelligence designation.

"I'm sorry, did you say level-two intelligence?"

"Of course," Kirian answered, raising an eyebrow. Then she smirked. "Oh, he didn't tell you, did he? Saved a lot of money on your salary by lying about your test scores." Kirian shook her head. "I should have shot him with a real gun."

Kirian ran to the elevator. Ari stood her ground. What was going on? She replayed the previous few minutes in her head. Something about Kirian looking at her watch alarm was starting to worry her. There were only two possibilities. Kirian was crazy, or Kirian was right. Even the thought of that made the room spin again. Was this planet really about to be deleted?

Kirian held the elevator doors open and yelled. "You're making this harder than it needs to be, Ari. We really have to hurry."

Ari heard her, but she needed a moment to think. After all, she'd just been fired for the first time ever. A new wave of wooziness washed over her as she remembered Mr. Brake and his threats. Even if Kirian wasn't right about the imminent deletion of the planet, actual security would likely arrive soon, and that was bad too.

For the first time in her life, Ari had to make a split-second decision. The only thing she could go on was instinct. She didn't like going on instinct. She realized with a jolt that she was overthinking a fight or flight response. Was that even possible?

"Now, Ari. Don't make me shoot you," Kirian shouted.

Ari made up her mind. It was a simple act, running to catch an elevator. Her body ran fast, but her mind moved even faster, objecting all the way down the hallway and into the elevator where she joined the visibly annoyed Kirian.

"Took you long enough," said Kirian, pushing the button for the lobby.

Ari, what have you done?

* * *

ARI'S MIND was still racing when the elevator dinged as they reached the ground floor. She followed Kirian, who confidently weaved her way through the crowd of business people and out through the main door.

Once outside, Ari stopped. What had been a beautiful, sunny day earlier had deteriorated into one that looked like the apocalypse. Black clouds filled the skies. Papers, pizza boxes, and articles of clothing blew by. There was an energy in the air Ari had never felt before, and a smell of static-charged electricity.

Kirian turned west. Ari followed, hurrying to catch up.

"What's going on?" Ari yelled into the wind. A tremor rolled beneath her feet. She wobbled, running faster to catch herself. The pavement rippled further down the street, causing her to become disoriented. "Kirian!"

Kirian slowed and turned to face her. "What?"

Somehow Ari hadn't expected that. And by the angry expression on Kirian's face, she figured asking her if she had seen the concrete ripple wasn't a good idea.

Kirian's left eye twitched. "Look, Ari, we have to get out of here now. Keep up."

The ground buckled beneath Ari's feet. This time a strange metallic roar accompanied it. She kept running. Then another quake knocked her off her feet.

"What is going on?" Ari asked while getting back up. "I've been here almost two years, and we've never once had a quake. There's almost no tectonic plate instability on this planet's surface."

"Nerd," Kirian replied.

Movement up high caught the corner of Ari's eye. She turned to face it and couldn't believe what she saw. It didn't make sense. Nothing made sense anymore. A giant Egyptian fox statue appeared to be walking on two legs through the middle of downtown. *What in stars?* Several parts of Ari's mind started to scream and argue with each other at the same time.

Kirian grabbed Ari by both shoulders.

Everything seemed to be happening in slow motion and none

of it felt real. Ari couldn't help but think that she was in a bad B-movie, and that she needed some popcorn.

Kirian shook her violently. It wasn't as fun as it looked in movies. "Ari, listen."

Ari snapped out of her daze. And now her arms hurt. "What?"

"We have to run. Now!" Kirian turned and darted like a deer through the now very busy city street, the lit ends of her dark hair trailing behind her dramatically.

Ari concentrated on following her. The simplicity of the task helped her to focus.

People were emptying out of buildings and flooding the streets. There was screaming and general mayhem and the smell of smoke. *Is this what happens when a planet gets deleted?*

Ari understood why they were running, but she couldn't figure out why she and Kirian were going in the opposite direction of everybody else. The main portals out of town were the other way.

Ari yelled. "Kirian, you're going the wrong way." Maybe Kirian had gotten turned around in the confusion.

"Trust me," said Kirian, slowing down just enough for Ari to hear her above the roar. "We're going the right way." She indicated to the crowd around them. "They're not going anywhere. I'll explain later."

Ari's phone chimed an emergency notification. She looked at it. "They closed all portals leaving the planet. How did you know they were going to do that? And what's going to happen to all of them?"

"Closing the portals is the standard planetary emergency procedure. And right now, my worry isn't them, it's us and getting to my portal. Fast."

"You have your own portal?" Ari asked.

"Shut up and run." Kirian set off running again, even faster than before. Ari struggled to keep up. They were making their way out of the city now, heading toward a dirt field bordered by scraggly trees.

Another metallic roar pierced the air. It reminded Ari of the soundtrack from a Godzilla movie. Every hair on her body stood up. She ran faster. Kirian stopped suddenly as they reached the trees and Ari nearly ran into her.

"Why are we stopping?"

"Oh, now you're in a hurry?" Kirian answered, poking through the trees. "Where is it?"

Another roar followed a new quake. It knocked them both off their feet.

Ari crawled over to Kirian. "No, really. What are we looking for?"

"My portal," Kirian replied, crawling in and around the strand of trees.

"What does it look like?" Ari asked.

"Like a shimmer in the light. My tracker says we're close. You have to look at exactly the right angle, or you can't see it. Otherwise, it would just get stolen, wouldn't it? Not to mention the fact that they're illegal. A-ha, there it is." She pointed at it triumphantly, still on her knees. "Let's go."

Ari saw it too. A blue-grey distortion in the area beside a small Oak. If Kirian hadn't pointed it out, Ari would have walked right over it.

"You had something to do with all of this, didn't you?" Ari didn't move. She wasn't ready to go through the portal with the stranger sent to kill her who was involved in the destruction of an entire planet.

Another roar ripped through the air. Another rampaging Egyptian Fox. Ari ducked down further. Where were they coming from?

Kirian blinked at her. "Yes, of course, I did. Can't we argue about this on the other side?" She pointed at the shimmer. "There's a lot less death and destruction over there."

"No." Ari defiantly sat down in the mud. She instantly regretted her decision. "Tell me the truth."

"Then you'll come through the portal?"

"Then I'll come through the portal." Her stubbornness was losing the inner battle with her will to survive, but her pride had jumped in on the tug of war. Her heart was beating fast, and she could no longer feel her body. *Is this what shock feels like?*

"Fine," Kirian whispered, crawling over to her. "I knew about it, but it wasn't my fault, ok?"

"How did you know?" Ari wanted more than anything to go through the portal. To be safe and to live. But the planet was being destroyed and nothing made sense. It didn't help that right now she was in a small field partially exposed to rampaging monsters that had apparently come out of nowhere.

Ari almost laughed out loud at the thought that if she were, in fact, in a bad monster movie, she'd probably know more about what was going on than she did right now.

"I knew," said Kirian, her face pale, "because I submitted the paperwork. And trust me, if we don't go now, we're going to have much bigger problems than giant foxes."

A shadow fell across the ground. Ari looked up. One of the monsters had found them. It was a giant Egyptian fox-like creature, like the others, and it roared down at them. The smell of iron, garbage, and death filled her nostrils.

Even though Ari could see its fox-like face peering down at her, she screamed, but couldn't move. Prey instinct had kicked in. A hand grabbed her arm and pulled her forward. Then, for a second, everything faded to black.

Chapter 3

Ari and Kirian fell through the portal.

Ari lay still and caught her breath. They were in a spaceship. The sounds of screaming and roaring were gone, replaced by the low hum of processors on the bridge of the craft. Stars shone through the windows. The distinct tang of stale, recirculated air filled her nostrils.

"Fleek!" Kirian yelled. "Fire in the hole." She turned to Ari. "Fire in the hole means the planet's going to blow up and we need to warp out of here now."

A tall and slender guy with blue lipstick and a blond Mohawk ran to the console and strapped himself into the pilot's chair. "Switching to manual," he said. "Navigation on screen." He didn't look like any pilot Ari had ever seen. She hoped he could actually fly this thing.

"Who's he?" Ari asked.

Kirian didn't answer; she grabbed onto a chair. Nearby explosions rocked the ship.

"Planet, on screen," Ari yelled. The console switched from the navigation coordinates to the planet they just left. The planet was on fire now and covered in smoke. Ari screamed.

Mohawk guy yelled too. For the screen to change back to navigation.

Another explosion rocked the ship. Then the gravity gave way, and Ari started floating. The floating wasn't so bad. Everything was calm, almost peaceful. Then she hit the floor, the ceiling, and the floor again in rapid succession. Ari hit the ground again hard. Only then did everything normalize.

Ari groaned, trying to catch her breath. "What happened?"

"Your planet blew up, and we warped away just in time. You're welcome," Kirian summed up.

"We?" said Mohawk. "I warped us out of there, thank you very much. So, who's this, another target?"

"Yes," Kirian said.

He unstrapped from the pilot seat and crossed the bridge to Ari, who still lay crumpled in the corner. "You're getting soft, Kirian. Hello, I'm Fleek."

"Nice to meet you," Ari managed weakly. She couldn't move. She had severe ship lag, and her whole body hurt, and there was a pounding pain in her head. "Another target, eh? So, did Kirian destroy your planet too?"

"Yes," said Fleek, "thank the stars. The place was a huge bore."

"It's not what you think," Kirian said defensively. "That was a completely different situation."

"Yeah," Fleek said, "my dad paid Kirian to save me, but I paid her more to tell him I was dead."

"That does sound different," Ari replied. "I just can't believe it's all gone."

"I didn't get the feeling you were going to miss that company or that boss." Kirian raised an eyebrow at Ari and turned to Fleek. "Her boss was a real piece of work. I mean, it's not like anyone appreciated her. I wouldn't think a human with your specifications would be stuck in a place like that."

Ari wanted to argue, but couldn't. "Okay, they were pretty

much jerks. Fine. That doesn't excuse blowing up an entire planet, and what about all those billions of lives?"

"Happens all the time, unfortunately," Kirian said. "It's the purpose of the Celestials. We do our jobs obtaining intelligence and files, commit the occasional assassination, and then she blows up the planet."

"She?"

"The Overseer herself, the Neon Octopus Overlord," Kirian said.

"Hang on," Ari said, "you're telling me that the most Efficient Being in the Galaxy, the Octopus Overlord herself, is behind all of this? Why?"

"No idea. That's what I'm trying to tell you," said Kirian, "I'm way down on the food chain here. I don't get explanations. I get orders."

Ari conceded the point. She only had one more question. "Don't think I'm ungrateful, but why did you save my life?"

Kirian ran a hand through her hair and sighed. Then she threw herself heavily into a nearby chair.

Ari managed with great effort to pull herself into a sitting position. "Hang on, two more questions," Ari corrected. "Where did the Egyptian fox-statue monsters come from?"

"I saved you because I need your help. And as to the fox monsters, they are called TPHWs or Temporarily Physical Holographic Weapons. They can take any form, they don't have to be foxes. The rumor is that only the Octopus herself can make the TMHWs work."

"No way," Ari said. "The technology you're talking about is not possible."

"Fine," Kirian said, "it's not possible. But I know you saw them yourself. Deal with it however you like."

Kirian was right. And Ari didn't feel like dealing with it at all right then. She changed the subject. "And now we're here on your fancy space ship with your..." Her gaze shifted from Kirian to Fleek.

"Ex," Kirian said.

"You don't have to say it like that," Fleek said, frowning.

"I didn't say it like anything."

"So why exactly," Ari interjected, "do you need my help?"

Kirian looked nervously from Fleek to Ari. Then she whispered, "I think I'm losing it." Kirian pointed at her own head. "I keep blacking out." Her face flushed. "And stealing things. I swear, it's not on purpose."

Ari was not expecting that at all. She had no idea how to respond. Luckily, Fleek jumped in.

"I'm telling you it's that hypnotherapist. You really should switch to mine. Mine doesn't use mind control. He also doesn't encourage petty theft."

Kirian drew the curved sword from somewhere inside her clothes and brandished it at Fleek menacingly. Then she stopped and held up her wrists to reveal identical wraparound metal bracelets. "I have no choice in the matter, do I? And as I keep pointing out, they are mandatory brainwashing sessions, not therapy."

Fleek took the sword brandishing in stride. He raised his hands at her. "I know that. I do. And I'm sorry. It's just that maybe if you saw my Oracle, he could offset some of what that nut case is doing to you."

"She wasn't always this jumpy," Fleek told Ari.

Ari climbed to her feet and stumbled to the bridge area before falling into a chair. "So, let me get this straight. Those bracelets are some sort of restraint?" Ari found this idea unlikely from a technology standpoint, and also from a legal one. "And you're forced into brainwashing sessions?"

Kirian nodded. “Company policy.”

“What company? Because that doesn't sound right at all.” Ari turned to face Fleek. "And you see an Oracle too? Where did you find yours?"

"On television. In infomercials that run around the clock," Fleek said cheerfully, ignoring Ari's eye roll.

Ari nodded and pointed at Fleek. "So, you are going to an Oracle that you found on television, and you're calling her brainwashing hypnotherapist a nutcase?"

"She's very judgy," Fleek said to Kirian.

* * *

A HAPPY RING tone chimed on the console.

"Finally," Fleek said, "it's my Oracle."

Ari turned with Kirian and Fleek to face the screen. A tall, dark-haired and bearded being appeared. He sat on a gaudy throne.

"Greetings, Oracle!" Fleek said cheerfully. "I was just telling Kirian here that she should switch to you instead of the awful being she's seeing now. He's brainwashing her."

"Just so you know," the Oracle said, "my rates have gone up since last time. And of course you should switch to me, um, Kirian. I assume Kirian is one of these two girls." He pointed a finger back and forth between Ari and Kirian.

"I'm Kirian," she said, waving, "Destroyer of Planets."

"Good for you," the Oracle replied. "I'm sure I can do a much better job than that other guy. You gotta be careful with brainwashing, it's a nasty business."

"You're telling me," Kirian mumbled.

"And what's with the other one?" the Oracle asked, indicating Ari. "Are we going to make this session a threesome?"

Fleek looked hopeful.

"No," Ari said. "We are not."

Kirian shook her head.

The oracle became distracted by somebody else, somebody off-screen that Ari couldn't see.

"Oi!" the Oracle yelled and stood up. He was looking and yelling at something off to his left. "Don't touch that. It's mine. How many times do I have to explain it to you..."

Ari studied the being on the screen carefully. The accent the Oracle used disappeared when he started yelling. He also seemed to forget, and then remember, that he was in the middle of a session.

"Apologies," he said, turning back to them with a cheesy bow before crossing to a mysterious looking machine. "So, what is the question for today, Fleek?"

"I've been wrestling with some personal and professional questions," Fleek answered. He eyed Ari and Kirian, obviously hoping for a little privacy.

Ari wasn't going anywhere and by the look of it, neither was Kirian.

Fleek continued speaking after shooting both of them a dirty look. "Well, it's the fractals." His face turned red. "I feel like they're telling me it's time. That the things that you and I have been discussing for the last year or so are there for the taking."

"You'll have to be more specific," the Oracle replied, "for the machine."

Fleek shot the girls another desperate, get-lost look before finally giving up. "Um, the music stuff," he said to the Oracle. "You know. Fame, fortune, rock and roll, all of it. Is it my time?"

The Oracle hit the button on the machine while Fleek droned on and on about music and fame and illegal amplifiers and such. In the end, the machine spat out some dice, and Fleek finally stopped talking. The Oracle glanced at them.

"So," Fleek asked, breathless in anticipation, "what do you have to say to all of that. Should I proceed?"

The Oracle looked at Fleek with a broad, predatory smile. He glanced down at the dice and then back up at Fleek. "Sure," he shrugged, "why not." This answer was followed very quickly by, "Look at the time, we'll catch up soon."

The screen faded to black.

Fleek wore a broad smile. "Yes," he said, adding a little fist pump.

Kirian spoke to Ari. "See? That Oracle guy's not serious at all, and I have a real problem."

The console played another jingle. This time it was the theme music for the Evil Emperor Xandorff from the Intergalactic Jannister television series.

"What in stars?" Ari asked.

Instead of answering her, Fleek sprinted across the room. He tackled her, sending them both underneath the console desk and out of view. Ari let out a pained groan.

From her vantage point on the floor, Ari could see Kirian sitting in her chair in front of the console. Fleek's eyes bulged out, and he stared wildly at Ari. He held a finger over his mouth, pleading for her to be quiet.

"Okay," Ari mouthed, "I get it already."

The voice broadcast through the speakers sounded calm. Too calm, it was creepy. Kirian jolted and buzzed in obvious discomfort at odd times during the conversation.

Ari nearly nodded off twice at the soothing tone. She shook her head to keep herself awake. Seeing Kirian jolt again, she realized with horror that Kirian was being intermittently zapped with electricity through her bracelets.

She turned to Fleek who shook his head and placed a finger over his mouth again.

Then the voice told Kirian she wouldn't consciously remember any of his instructions when awake. After a snap of fingers, the voice disappeared.

Ari and Fleek chanced a peek at the screen to make sure he was indeed gone. The screen was blank again.

"What in stars was that?" Ari asked, emerging from beneath the console.

"That's what I've been trying to tell you. He's the guy that's making her steal, except she doesn't remember any of it afterward."

Ari wouldn't have believed it if she hadn't seen it herself.

"You can never let him see you," Fleek said to Ari. "Never make eye contact, or he'll have you, too."

"How do you know that?" Ari asked, trying not to let on how much the two of them were creeping her out.

"I was in the galley when this new hypnotherapist came in a few months ago. I could only hear him, and I'm pretty sure that's why I'm okay. He kept asking if anyone else was on the ship. You have to understand, Kirian's first hypnotherapist was a mostly harmless guy; just rah-rah go Celestial type of stuff. Then this guy showed up, and it got serious really fast."

"Hang on," Ari said. "Celestial? Actual Celestial? As in secret government conspiracy stuff? That's a myth. Like purple spotted wormholes or Space Seahorses."

"Hey," said Kirian, regaining consciousness in her chair and groaning, "I've seen both of those things."

The console buzzed to life again, this time with no notification song.

Ari glanced at Fleek. "What, you're not going to tackle me this time? How do you two ever get any work done with these constant interruptions?"

"I'm a musician," Fleek answered. "I work odd hours. And trust me, this is not a typical day."

"Kirian, listen," the handsome figure on the screen whispered.

"Drexyl, be a dear and bring me the soap," said a strange female voice offscreen.

"In a minute," the figure on the screen fake-cheerfully yelled back.

The guy Ari assumed was Drexyl faced them once more.

"Look. She's in the shower. I don't have much time. She's terminating the Celestial program. I don't know exactly when, yet. But when she does, she's going to delete all the Celestials. You have to get out of there, Kirian."

Kirian narrowed her eyes at him and held up her wrists. "How in stars name am I supposed to do that, Drexyl? I'm a prisoner too."

"Drexyl, what's the holdup with the soap?" the female voice off screen yelled.

Drexyl shook his head. "I have to go."

Once again, the console faded to black and then eventually to clear, allowing a beautiful view of the stars. Everyone just sat quietly for awhile.

"I feel like I got here at a bad time," Ari said, at last, breaking a very uncomfortable silence.

Chapter 4

"No!" Kirian yelled, thumping the console in a delayed reaction after Drexyl disappeared. "Come back. I didn't get to ask him to tell that stupid Octopus to lay off the brainwashing. Those sessions," she shook her head, causing a cascade of light to flicker from the ends of her hair. "I'm starting to lose it. Fleek's right, this new CBC guy is messing me up. I mean, I think he is. I'm not even sure anymore."

"New CBC guy?"

"The Celestial Brainwashing Coordinator. The guy brainwashing me. That's his actual title. If I don't keep the appointments, they zap me full of electricity and then hunt me down. It wasn't like this before. I remember the old coordinator. Jake. Fun guy. But then it all changed. Now I don't remember anything afterward." Kirian swallowed. "Well, there is something I remember. The nightmares I've been having."

The flash of fear that Ari saw behind Kirian's eyes scared her.

"What nightmares?" Ari asked.

"Every night it's the same thing. It's stupid, really. You wouldn't believe me if I told you."

"Try me," Fleek and Ari said together.

Ari shot him a dirty look.

"Jinx," he said.

Kirian ran her fingers through her hair again as she paced around the room. She stopped and looked at Ari. "Okay, I'll tell you, but only because you might be able to help. I hope."

"Can you just spit it out?" Fleek asked.

"Fine. Every night lately, I dream about a giant Praying Mantis species. He eats beings alive. I wish I could get the images out of my head. Why would I dream about that?"

Fleek closed his mouth and took a step back. Ari was unable to hide a quick intake of breath.

"Don't even say that," Ari whispered. "Those things aren't allowed within a hundred light years of our galaxy. Arcturis is a safe place."

The very thought of a Preying Mantis species terrified Ari. Maybe she was better off getting away from this space ship and finding a new planet and a new job. Something far away from basket case warriors and evil Octopus Overlords.

"I'll tell you what," Ari said. She went to Kirian and put a hand on her shoulder. She didn't like the situation she was currently in, but no harm could come from calming the girl with the deadly weapons.

"I remember the ring tone that sounded when the CBC guy showed up. I'll just listen in on what's going on next time. Maybe I can even record it for you. It'll probably make more sense in context. I'll even take a peek, so you know exactly what he looks like. I'm sure it's a perfectly normal being, not a giant Praying Mantis. Then we'll all feel much better. Ok? How does that sound?"

"No," Fleek said, "you can't look at him."

"I'm not going to look at him," Ari replied. "I'm going to Medusa him. I'll look at him through a mirror, that way if he is a crazy being with brainwashing power I'll be safe."

"That's genius."

"It's what I do," Ari answered, waving off the compliment.

"I don't know," said Fleek. "You think it'll work?"

"I do," Ari replied. "Believe me; these things usually end up being more normal and less scary the more scrutiny they get. So that's just what we're going to do. Okay, Kirian?"

The console beeped.

"What now," Ari asked. "Another therapy session?"

"No," Kirian answered, tapping information into the console. "Apparently, I've been given another Celestial job. That's strange because it's a much quicker turnaround than usual. Drexyl might be right about the timeline of the deletion of the Celestials."

Ari swallowed hard. She wanted to help, but she might be running out of time. "Which planet?"

Kirian finished reading the information. "It's called Reptar."

Chapter 5

"Thaara," Soda muttered, entering the main room again after her shower.

"You said that was the message on the television earlier, what does it mean?" Drexyl asked while toweling off the ends of her tentacles.

"It's a code word. It means 'The Staars are looking for you. The staars will find you."

Drexyl's neck hair stood on end at the mention of staars. "How do you know that?"

"Because," she answered, "I'm the one they're looking for."

Drexyl dropped the towel. "You have actual Staar bounty hunters looking for you? Like in the horror movies? Why? And what will they do to any innocent bystander prisoners who happen to be in the vicinity? I mean, because I've heard stories."

"Yeah, the Staars are jerks," Soda answered. "Oh, and mistakes were certainly made, Drexyl. Let's just say I had a very reckless youth. If only I could go back in time."

"You'd change it and not have terrifying Staar bounty hunters after you?"

"Oh no," she said, "I'd do the whole thing all over again. Right now, if I could. I had no end of fun. Those were the days. In fact, it all started with a death sentence, one that I received unfairly might I add, in a tiny system of planets where I grew up. Those were the days. And with that sort of thing hanging over your head, well, it makes you nervous. That's when I decided to chase after the immortality."

"That's right!" Drexyl said, picking up the towel. "You're immortal now. So, they can't kill you. Then what are you worried about, anyway? It's the rest of us that need to be scared."

"Don't you ever listen to me? It was only afterward that I realized how many things can be even worse than death. And believe me, those are the kinds of Staars who know how to dish it out."

"So, what are you going to do?" Drexyl asked. Despite being a prisoner, he looked around the room with the aim of making new security suggestions.

Instead of answering, Soda began to pace, slithering back and forth across the floor.

"Well, let's see. I stepped up the completion and deletion of Celestial. That ought to keep those Staars from poking their nose too far into the comings and goings of this galaxy. Hopefully. You see, one of the missions of Celestial all this time has been to rid the galaxy of Palladium."

"Palladium? Who cares? It's not even worth anything." Drexyl walked around, double checking that the doors were locked and bolted.

"Correct. It's not appreciated at all here," Soda said. "That's how I've gotten away with everything so far. That and the sucker contract those Intergalactic Council yahoos signed. Anyway, Palladium is an element used by the Staars to communicate. If you get rid of the Palladium; then they can't talk to each other. Even if one finds you, it can't call for help. Is it ideal? No. But it's a lot better than the alternative. Next, we'll have to figure out the best way to safeguard ourselves in the meantime."

"Yeah," said Drexyl quickly. "What's that plan?"

"No idea," said Soda, yawning. "I'll have to sleep on it."

Drexyl's shoulders slumped. He needed her to come up with a very good plan. And soon.

Chapter 6

Ari emerged from the space ship blinking into a beautiful, sunny day. It was warm. Not oppressively warm. Happy warm. The kind of warm that made her want to lay in a hammock and take a nap. She yawned and stretched out on the planet's dusty surface, resting her head in her arms.

"Ok," said Kirian, snapping a small Biome Analyzer closed and placing it back in her pocket. "There might be a tad too much carbon monoxide here for you. We gotta move. I still don't know what it is that you're doing here on-planet with me."

Kirian helped Ari up, and together they moved closer to the city.

"I'm going to do some research. See what I can find out," Ari said, yawning. "Maybe I can help you with your handcuffs."

"Restraints."

"Or figure out how to break the hypnotherapy spell. Or maybe just stop the Overseer from destroying this fine planet."

"You don't know anything about this planet." Kirian objected.

"That's true, but I have a good feeling about it. And besides, it beats staying on the ship."

As they approached the city, the carbon monoxide concentration fell, and Ari started feeling better. She entered the large metropolitan area wide-eyed, taking it all in.

Kirian stopped outside a purple skyscraper in the middle of the bustling downtown.

“Why have we stopped?” Ari asked, staring up at the skyscraper looming over them. A sign over the main entrance said: "Reptar Planetary Federal Building" in happy, giant purple letters. Ari gave them credit for at least trying to put a positive spin on the whole planetary civil service idea. And also, for their obvious fondness for the color purple.

"This is my next mission," Kirian answered. "This is how Celestial works. The system automatically creates a resume for whatever it is these people need." She waved at the building. "If I already have a job when I get here, then it streamlines the process and makes them less suspicious of me, making my job easier."

"And you need the fake resume because you don't actually know anything about civil service," Ari continued.

"Exactly. Because I don't, in fact, know anything about it,” Kirian answered. “And furthermore, I don't care. For me, the whole thing's just a cover anyway."

Ari continued to take in the sights and sounds around her. They had arrived in Reptar's capital city in rush hour, judging by the traffic. The beings surrounding them were humanoid-looking, but with some notable exceptions, one of which included assorted extra digits on their extremities.

"Anyway, your resume got accepted just fine, Ari. Welcome aboard, Level eight Specialist Data Consultant."

Ari's eyes widened. "You got me a promotion?"

"No, you got you a promotion. It's your resume. When you said you wanted to come on-planet with me, I forwarded yours along with mine and they accepted us both."

Ari didn't want to admit it, but she was glad to be here. She was excited about being on another planet with a new job and promotion, even if it was only temporary.

They entered the building, and she followed Kirian through the labyrinthine interior until they reached Ari's new office.

"Have fun," said Kirian, and then she was gone.

Ari's new boss stopped by a few minutes later to introduce himself. He was taller than Ari. His species was very tall with elongated limbs and a head that was too small for his body. He had thinning brown hair and large expressive eyes.

"Hello," he said, coming around the desk to extend a hand. "Welcome to data crunching. Your resume was most impressive. We were lucky to find you. How did your last employer manage to let you get away?"

Ari took a deep breath. She didn't want to think of her old boss or her last planet right now, or what Kirian was doing at this moment. She decided to do what she could for these good, kind people who happened to appreciate intelligent new employees. There should be more of that in the universe, not less.

"No matter," he continued. "You see, an issue has come up. And so far, none of us can make heads or tails of it. We were hoping that an experienced traveler of the galaxy such as yourself could help us figure it out."

Ari swallowed. She wondered if Kirian had, in fact, enhanced her resume. *It doesn't matter where I have or haven't been,* she thought. *I'm very good at my job.*

"I do love a good mystery," she answered.

KIRIAN DROPPED Ari off and set the coordinates for that office on her watch. Then she raced to another floor of the building, so she could find her own new boss, who showed her around and gave her the passwords for her work pod. Formalities over with, she went to work.

The alternate passwords given to her by the Celestial agency gained her access to all of the databases. It was probably traceable, but it didn't matter. By the time the locals had a clue what she was up to she'd be long gone, as would the planet, probably.

She navigated into the main system, then the shadow system, then into security. *Stars. Hard copies?* Who puts important information on hard copies anymore? What was wrong with these people? *Things just got more complicated.*

She patted the outside of her jacket pocket and located her sleep ray gun. It was her failsafe along with the Stingr Swords in her pants pockets. Right where they were supposed to be. *Good.*

The Stingr Swords were custom-made and collapsed down to the size of lipstick containers. It meant she could travel with them anywhere. Of course, she also had her curved metal sword, which didn't say much for local security.

There was nothing to do but make her way to the basement and face the Keeper of the Files. She headed out of her cubicle into the hallway and ran right into a tall, elongated being with an unstylish fish tie. She hoped for his sake that he was wearing it ironically. Fish Tie Guy stared down at her. He had a stack of papers in his arms.

"Good. New girl. Arrange these files for me." He looked at his watch. "It's almost lunch. Be back to get them soon." He leaned his head down to scowl at her. "Don't screw it up. If those files are not right after lunch, I won't have time to fix them." He made a threatening gesture and was gone.

Kirian watched him walk away. She ran her tongue along her upper left canine tooth. Then she imagined at least four different ways to kill him in her head. The last one made her laugh.

What have I ever done to deserve this stupid, hard-copy planet? I don't have time for this.

She was left standing with her pent-up anger and a stack of files. She had no idea what Fish Tie Guy was talking about, and there was no way she'd have the hard copies before lunch was over. The only option she had was to make her way back to Ari and hope she could help.

* * *

FROM HER CORNER office on the eighty-third floor, Ari had a beautiful view of the city. Even after she won the Jawsdon Genius award on her home planet, this kind of office had still been out of her reach at her last job.

She sighed contentedly, reached for her coffee mug, and mulled over the hard copies of data her boss had given her. The "coffee" was thick, not too sweet, and had a little something extra in it. The best Ari could describe it was a sort of cross between coffee, chai tea, and a something else she couldn't identify. It made her warm and happy, and the taste reminded her a little bit of rum.

The paper felt good in her hand. Strong and sturdy. She studied it by the natural light flooding through her window while lounging back, not bent over the artificial light of her computer screen. Hard copies. Something about it was just so soothing.

Kirian appeared in the doorway, startling her. "Ari. Finally. Even with coordinates, this building is a maze."

"Kirian." Ari was happy to see her. "How is your morning going? Can you believe this office? Hey, I get the feeling you enhanced my resume for this position."

"Yes, you're welcome."

"No, you wait a minute. This thing they gave me to figure out. It's hard. That's why they requisitioned a level eight associate. I was a level five and a half, you know."

Kirian slumped into the chair opposite Ari and next to the window. "Look. I worked at your previous office briefly. You think anybody there was smarter than you?"

"Not remotely."

"See?" Kirian said. "You'll be fine. Doesn't matter anyway. We'd be gone already if this stupid planet didn't keep hard copies of everything."

"I happen to like hard copies. Hey, Kirian. Let me know if this planet is going to be destroyed. Because, if not, I may just stay. I can do all the research from here instead of on the ship."

Kirian looked wounded. "Fine." She showed the stack of papers in her hand to Ari. "Some guy who hates me told me to organize these. Soon, or he'd kill me or something."

"Doubt it," said Ari, accepting the papers and inspecting them. "Oh, this'll only take five minutes...he just wants you to organize them according to date and amount and..." She looked up, and Kirian was gone.

Ari sighed and wished Kirian would stop doing that.

Chapter 7

For Fleek, it all started with Kirian being gone so much. When she was off doing Celestial stuff, Fleek would watch mathematical fractals in secret, a practice forbidden in all of the planets in the known galaxy. The law came from the Neon Octopus Overlord herself. Nobody knew exactly why. At least not in the corners of the internet he had searched.

The policy had only been in place for a couple of centuries. Fleek was, in his heart, a musician. And musicians were supposed to be rebels. Illegal fractals seemed like a good place to start, and being a galaxy-class hacker; he knew exactly where to find them. Oh yes, finding forbidden fruit on the dark net was his forte. That, and the video game Low Down Nemesis. Nobody beat him at that.

The fractals fascinated him at first, but then the whole thing had taken off into addiction territory, with Fleek developing an eye twitch if Kirian was on-ship for too long.

Only then did the fractals make their way into his music. Two obsessions that worked hand in glorious, addiction-fueled hand until he finished the song.

The song was perfect. He knew exactly what he had to do

next because the fractals "told" him. They said the time had come for the song to burst forth into the galaxy. Or something like that. It was more of a feeling than actual communication.

And he knew it was dangerous. More dangerous than being a hacker. More dangerous than being saved at the last minute by a hot girl Celestial as the planet he was on was about to be destroyed. If nothing else, Fleek had been on a lucky streak lately.

The problem was what to do about the danger part. Hire a bunch of private security like a big baby? Not going to happen. Then he got the idea. He would form a band. It was his song, and he would sing, of course. But the song needed plenty of other instruments. Then he could broadcast it to the galaxy. Illegally, spectacularly, and pirate-style, like a hacker who'd faked his own death should.

That's the way to make a name for yourself, Fleek. And isn't that the whole point of it?

He would have to find others like himself, music lovers. Except these would be hard-core and dangerous ones who also wanted to fake their deaths. Beings who wanted out of their boring normal worlds and into the world of music and art and space-legend. Beings like him. They would also be capable of protecting him if trouble showed up. Win-win.

Thoughts of fame, glory, and musical immortality filled his head as he dialed.

* * *

"Oi, who's this?" Carpe answered his cell. He looked around self-consciously. Luckily, nobody was paying attention to him. He hated getting phone calls at work. And he was always at work. He even hated digging the stupid thing out of his pocket and putting it on his face like he was some oozing commuter in a suit.

If he wanted to be some poor sap tethered to his phone he

wouldn't be Regal, then, would he? Regal being the most violent organized crime syndicate in his part of the galaxy. He listened to see who was on the other end of the line so he could figure out the most appropriate way to insult and then hang up on them.

Screams filled the room, which interrupted the sound of the person on the other end of the line. Carpe couldn't hear, and he wasn't about to ask the warlord to keep the interrogation down. He stood, stomped into the bathroom, and shut the door. He sat down heavily and focused.

"Now then. I didn't get any of that, mate. You have fifteen seconds to tell me why I shouldn't trace this call, find your refracting ass and black hole you right back into the nearest star, along with your phone."

Satisfied, he took a breath and listened. This call was different. The guy on the other end was the first one to ever make it past fifteen seconds.

* * *

FLEEK WAS JAZZED. The conversation was going well. "I found your musical recordings. You're talented."

"That's not possible," Carpe said. "None of my recordings are available to the public."

"Your bass version of How Deep are my Synapses was masterful. I want to offer you a job."

"I got a job, ain't I? I'm Regal. If you were here, I'd rip your arms off just to show you. You have no idea what I'm like or what kind of people I work for."

"Oh, I've heard of them, alright." *It's why I'm contacting you,* Fleek thought, but he didn't say it. "And I'm not just offering you a new job. I'm offering you a new life. Nobody who plays as well as you do can ever be truly happy not playing."

"Even if I wanted to drop everything and become a musician —and I don't—why would I trust you?"

Fleek smiled. This was his favorite part. He ran his hands through his long Mohawk. He did this often to remind himself of who he was before, who he was now, and who he planned on becoming. "Because, mate. I faked my own death. And now I create music full time. As much as I want. On a Celestial ship."

"You're lying."

"It's the truth," Fleek replied. "And that's not even the best part. Listen."

Fleek hit go on his communicator, and let the song play. The song would speak for itself. The song was the key. Anybody who could listen to the song and walk away? Well, they weren't destined for greatness. They simply weren't worthy. Fleek waited for the song to finish.

"Well?"

"I'll admit. I've never heard anything like it." Fleek heard him sniffle. "What do you expect me to do? Just walk away from everything? You know what these guys'll do to me?"

"Oh, one more thing. And I think this will help you to decide," Fleek said. "I do understand. I'm going to tell you something I shouldn't. Something that could easily get me killed. My real name, my truest identity so far. Are you ready?"

"Sure. Go ahead, mate."

"I'm Fractal."

There was laughter on the other end of the line. "There's no way you're Fractal, mate."

"I wouldn't be so sure I was a good judge of things if I were sentimental enough to make my password the birthday of the pet snake I had when I was seven years old," Fleek replied and then waited.

"How could you possibly..."

It was true. Before Fleek started watching Fractals, he had been one of the top five hackers in the galaxy. It was one of the few secrets his dad hadn't ferreted out when he'd unleashed the army of private investigators.

Hacker Fractal was wanted on fifteen planets. There was no way even his dad could have cut a deal on all of them; nobody had that much leverage.

Unable to catch him or figure out his identity, the policing authorities had finally given up and put a price on his head so high, they figured someone would turn him in eventually.

Even though he had now faked his own death, lived on the ship with a Celestial agent believed to be a legend, and changed his appearance so completely that he no longer recognized himself in the mirror (*hey handsome*), it was still a huge risk telling people his secret identity.

"I'm recruiting my band. My crew," continued Fleek. "I'm inviting you to join, and I'm only asking once. After this, I'm going to disappear. What'll it be, Carpe? You in or you out?"

Fleek waited. He didn't want to deny the guy the chance to think it over. It was no small thing to abandon a life, although if Fleek knew then what he knew now, he'd have done it a lot sooner.

"Okay," Carpe said, "I'm in. Send me the coordinates."

Fleek smiled and made a triumphant fist pump. He had gotten to the end of the spiel more than half a dozen times, and this was the first time it had actually worked.

Chapter 8

With her boss at lunch, clubbing baby seals, or whatever he was currently doing—and Ari fixing the files, Kirian figured she had a window to sneak into central records and find what she needed. This planet was getting on her nerves.

When she got there, a large reptilian creature sat at the desk, eating a take-out container in which the contents were moving. Its tongue darted in and out of the container while it casually read what looked to be an entertainment magazine.

Oh no. Anything but reptilian. It was one of Kirian's few fears. Once you cross a reptilian, you have no way of knowing how it will turn out. They were as deadly and obnoxious as they were unpredictable.

"Can I help you?" it said it without looking up. It turned a page.

"Oh, hello. You must be the Records Keeper." In Kirian's experience, planets with hard copies usually had powerful beings guarding said records, even from their employees. It didn't make sense to Kirian, but then again, she was the entire reason for the extra security. For this, though, she took absolutely no responsibility. They did their job; she did hers.

“Who are you?” it asked.

Kirian met its cold, black eyes. She swallowed at the sight of rows of white teeth unable to be contained by the creature's face. One tooth that had poked free of its lip had something small and black wriggling in it.

"I'm Kirian." She hadn't bothered changing her name this time, having no idea the mission would take so long because they didn't have electronic copies of documents. "I'm new here, you see, and they sent me to..."

"ID badge."

"Yes, but I only need a few minutes to grab..."

"Nobody gets into Central Records." The Reptile spoke slowly, staring her down, memorizing her face for future encounters. "And I mean nobody. Not without an ID badge."

Stars. There was no way the sleep ray gun would work on its thick skin, and no way it wouldn't love to chomp her into oblivion if she tried.

"And technically," it added for effect, "I'm allowed to eat anyone that tries."

Sounds about right. Kirian stomped off.

Hard copies. Reptilians. It was this sort of job that gave Celestials such a short life expectancy. And her time was running out. Kirian's shoulders sagged. She could do nothing except go back to her cubicle and find out how to get an ID badge. A job hadn't gone south this fast in years.

* * *

ARI LEFT her office and crossed the hallway to see her boss. She had a file in her hand opened to page 5,394. She knocked on the door.

"Come in. Oh, it's you, Ari. I didn't expect to see you for a while; it's quite the odd puzzle that we have you working on."

Ari entered and sat. "It's true. In fact, I was wondering, are you entirely sure about these stats?"

"Way ahead of you," he chuckled, "I had accounting check them three times before I even advertised for your position."

Ari mulled this over. "It's just that what's happening with these numbers can't be right. And if my theory is correct, it isn't legal, either."

"Oh," said the boss, rubbing his chin with his hand, "a theory. I'd love to hear it."

The turn of the conversation caught Ari completely by surprise. Nobody at her last job was the least bit interested in any anomalies she found in the myriad accounting, security, and interplanetary commerce reports she had access to. In fact, it was quite the opposite. She was used to hearing the equivalent of 'shut your pie hole.'

Ari stared up into those giant eyes and decided she wanted to be a little more certain.

"And I will tell you," she began, "but, let me just triple check the results, okay? Especially since my working theory isn't going to win us any friends. I want to be sure before we go shaking any palm trees that we aren't going to be dropping coconuts on our heads."

"That's my girl," he said, waving a hand with a pencil attached to it. "Better safe than sorry, that's what I always say. But I want to know just as soon as you're ready, ok?"

Ari liked him. They were getting along just fine.

"Hey, by the way, what's this coffee-like drink you guys have? It's delicious."

He burst into laughter, clapping his hands and pointing to her. "This one, level eight, pretending she's never had rum coffee before."

Ari smiled and played along. It was very different from the boring coffee on her last planet. Exploring the galaxy was turning out better than she expected.

* * *

KIRIAN WORE the shiny ID badge around her neck with a lanyard that the new-hire office had given her.

After collecting the ID, she had given Fish Tie Guy his papers; all organized the way he wanted, thanks to Ari. He had grunted at her and scurried off to a meeting. *You're welcome.*

She psyched herself up to go back to Central Records. *I can do this. I can march right in there and grab those stupid hard copies and get the hell off of this planet.*

Kirian smiled. For once, the scenes of destruction and craziness would make sense. That'll teach this planet for not having digital copies of sensitive information.

She thought about the hateful reptilian still in her way. She didn't want to do hand to hand combat with that thing. Because she would probably lose. But she was also running out of time.

Think.

One of the few weaknesses in the reptilian creatures was an intense sensitivity to light. It was a double pain in the neck when coupled with the fact that Kirian would need lots of light to find the files she was after. Management obviously kept the whole records department several shades darker than necessary or legal because nobody wanted to piss it off.

Lightbulb. Literally. She had an idea.

She tapped into her communicator and accessed her super bright, LED, ultraviolet Unmasker 3000. One blast on high, and the records keeper reptilian would be flailing around for at least five minutes, unable to see anything beyond muted shapes.

That thought made her laugh out loud. Of course, if the reptilian did manage to shake it off and locate her, she'd be dead. Still, it was worth a try, especially as a firm plan B. Plan A was to flash a smile and a legitimate security badge, and sweet talk her way in. Confidence coursed through her as she approached the desk. She was an official employee now. There was no reason for this not to work.

Chapter 9

Floyd sat hunched over the paper on his desk. He worked with his head down, and his arms at an angle until the paperwork was finished. Then he swiveled his head in practiced movements around the walls of his office, which was nearly but not completely covered in mirrors.

Satisfied, he put down the pencil and checked his watch. Excellent. Nearly six o'clock. He stood and walked out to the front desk where his receptionist, Rachel, was sitting.

He could have buzzed in his next meeting, like his colleagues would have done, but it simply wasn't his style. When he had sensitive appointments, he always wanted to see exactly what he was getting into.

He glanced at and then ignored the large, angry, oafish being standing over Rachel and trying to intimidate her. Superficially humanoid, he looked hairy, with pointy ears and long fingernails. Dreadful. His gaze returned to Rachel.

"How are you, Rachel? Big plans for tonight?"

"Actually," she beamed, "I have a date."

"Of course you do. And he's a lucky guy. This is my last appointment for the day. You go ahead and take off. I'll lock up."

"Are you sure? I mean, I can stay if you need me."

She looked a little worried. She's so sweet to be concerned.

"No need to worry about me, my dear. Trust me; I'll be right behind you. You have fun, okay? Stay safe. I'll see you first thing Monday morning."

Rachel gathered her things and headed for the door. Floyd waved and then turned his attention to the angry, hulking wolf-man.

"Right this way," Floyd said, directing wolf-man to his office, "I understand you have some complaints."

"Got that right. This company has the worst customer service in the galaxy. Hypno-therapy my thorax."

Must be some sort of slang, he thought. This hairy guy didn't have a thorax.

Floyd closed his office door for privacy. Sometimes these types of appointments got contentious. They both sat.

"So," said Floyd with a smile, "tell me your troubles, and I'll see what I can do to help."

Hairy Guy set off on an epic rant. Blah, blah, wife left him, kids won't speak to him, random children kick him in the street. Boring stuff, really.

Floyd had to force himself to nod randomly to stay awake and to keep Hairy Guy talking. The whole thing was just a play for time anyway, to see how long Hairy Guy could go on talking while the building emptied out. At long last, hairy guy finally took a breath.

"Okay, then," Floyd jumped in. "What I hear you saying is that this whole seemingly unrelated and frankly bizarre sequence of events is the fault of the..." Floyd paused to check a calendar on his desk, tapping it when he found the correct entry. "Oh yes, here it is. You're advancing the theory that all of these problems are solely the result of four hypnotherapy sessions over the last two weeks? Is that it?"

Hairy Guy's face turned red as Floyd raised an eyebrow indicating the implausibility of what he was suggesting.

"Well, it's somebody's fault, ain't it?"

Hairy Guy was right, of course. Spot on. It was the fault of the hypnotherapy sessions. Floyd risked a smile. In fact, it was proof positive that the targeted experiments were working to perfection.

And by the sheepish expression on his hairy face, the side effects were so outlandish and unlikely that not only would the complaints not hold up in court, it was clear that none of the victims would ever dare take it that far.

Floyd leaned forward and steepled his long fingers. "I can tell," he began, "that things aren't going particularly well for you right now."

"Got that right."

"And I'm pretty sure I have a solution for you. Something that will solve all of your problems, once and for all."

"About time."

"But first, you need to know one thing about me. My name's not Floyd."

Not-Floyd flickered. He knew this because the mirrors covering the walls of his office were there so he could watch everything—his own transformation, the terror of the victim, everything—from multiple angles.

After the flicker, he was no longer a mousy, suit-wearing average Joe; he was a giant Praying Mantis- Mantix species, whose head nearly bumped the ceiling. He glanced down behind the desk where a fresh tarp was laid out on the floor.

All of not-Floyd's attention was now focused on the soon-to-be victim. Hairy guy sat there terrified and frozen in place, eyes open wide and unblinking.

Drat. No fun at all. Run, darn you. Make a dash for the door. At least dart out somewhere.

Not-Floyd stood, arms poised, head twitching from left to right, waiting for his prey to act.

Finally, Hairy Guy broke out of his stunned state and scrambled toward the door. Not Floyd's giant pincers snatched him up and pulled him behind the desk. The prey was screaming now, but not for long.

As usual, Not-Floyd started at the top, with the head, the noisy part of the victim. The screams turned to gurgling and then stopped altogether.

"See?" Not-Floyd said as the gurgling died down, “I was right. You'll never again have to worry about what's troubling you."

Feeling helpful, Not-Floyd wrapped the rest of the body in the tarp for later and pushed it out of view. Someone knocked on the door. He wasn’t expecting that.

"Just a minute," he called out as cheerfully as he could despite the surprise interruption. His heart was beating at twice the normal rate. By this time the building was usually empty. He wondered if he could even eat again this close to the first victim. He transformed into Floyd again and took a seat behind his desk, pretending to stare at the computer.

"Come in," he called as he glanced around at the mirrors. There was blood on his face. The door opened as he snatched a tissue and dabbed the blood away. A janitor entered.

"Yes?" Floyd asked.

"I thought I heard screaming," the white-faced janitor stammered, looking around the office.

"Oh no," Floyd laughed, "that was just me. I'm afraid I got a look at last month's profit margin. Grim numbers, those. I apologize, I didn't know anyone else was within earshot. Aaaahhh," Floyd said in a mock scream, flailing his arms a little and vamping up the moment. "You get it, am I right?"

The janitor backed out of the room and closed the door.

In the silence that followed, Floyd took a deep, cleansing

breath. He glanced at his computer, and saw that there were new Celestial reports.

Yes, things were working out nicely. Why find and train your own evil army when there's a sucker Octopus with one of her own just waiting to be hijacked. Celestial was a fantastic find.

The former Celestial Brainwashing Coordinator, Jake, was all too easy to dispose of. Then Floyd simply stole and embellished Jake's resume and got the job.

Floyd rubbed his hands together. Where he was from, there was an art to conquering galaxies. There were style points awarded for doing as little actual work as possible, and everything was going according to plan. He leaned back in his chair with satisfaction.

Then he saw another notification from the Neon Octopus Overlord. He scanned it. It was a deletion notice. There would be two more Celestial missions. Then the whole program would be terminated along with the Celestials themselves. He re-read it. Why in stars would the stupid octopus do that? What was she thinking?

Maybe it was a mistake. How dare she kill the secret army he was so close to stealing? Floyd stared at the floor. He still had to clean up the blood and the mess, but he'd just finished eating and was tired. Housework would have to wait. And now, on top of everything else, he had to confront the octopus too. His to-do list was filling up fast, which was bad. Floyd prided himself on getting everybody else to do his dirty work.

Oh well. It's all temporary. The minute I take control, I won't have to do anything at all. Ever.

Chapter 10

As Kirian approached, the reptilian was sitting in the same spot, with a new magazine about architecture. The box of wriggling food was gone.

"Hello. Kirian again. Remember me? I think the two of us may have gotten off on the wrong foot. Oh look, architecture." Kirian forced a smile and pointed at the magazine. "I also find that subject fascinating."

Cold black eyes looked up and followed her around. Kirian realized she was pacing.

"As you can see," Kirian pressed on, "I have a brand-new ID badge. Told you. A small oversight from a new hire."

It bothered Kirian that the reptilian hadn't said anything, but she convinced herself she was being paranoid. "I'm just going to head back there and get to work." She waved a piece of paper around. "I have a list of files to grab, and then I'll be out of your, uh, hair." She chuckled at that last part.

Reptilians don't have hair.

Kirian waited in silence for a sign that it was going to let her pass without attempting to eat her. Moving forward tentatively, she orbited around it, heading toward the records area. She clutched the flashlight in her jacket pocket just in case.

Whew.

Once inside, records storage was as expected. It was huge, spread out over several loosely connected rooms, and dimly lit.

Stars, how do these idiots find anything?

According to the schematics she had brought up on her computer earlier, the first file would be in a back room off to the left.

Once at the indicated location, she searched the walls in vain for additional light switches before giving up.

Kirian pulled out her flashlight and adjusted the beam to its lowest possible setting. It still gave off plenty of light. She'd save the high power in case she needed it later. The first document she needed was KH763JN.

Yes. There it was. She digitized and uploaded it with her hand-held and carried on in search of the next document.

OPL98IUI.

The search brought her to a ladder in the middle of a large room that smelled of old pages, sweat, and disinfectant. She climbed it and propped the flashlight on an upper step. Her eye caught the gleam of her bracelet, reminding her she was a prisoner despite all appearances. She shook her head. Nobody ever said life was fair, Kirian. Just get on with it.

Finding the second file, she rechecked her watch. At least she was almost done. She uploaded it and slid down the ladder to the floor.

One more file to go.

RWE010XS.

Stars, that's in the other room, the one off to the right.

She listened at the entrance before proceeding. Silence.

Good.

She opened the door leading to the other records room and began to tiptoe across.

Halfway there, the reptilian appeared in the center of a group of half a dozen armed guards watching her sneak across.

When did they get here? Kirian wondered if they were this suspicious of all new hires or only potential agents out to destroy the planet. Why hadn't they just charged in to attack her? Why lie in wait like a bunch of high schoolers pulling a prank?

The reptilian charged her. Its mouth was wide open. White teeth glistened in the dimly lit room.

Stars.

The other security guards weren't there to attack; they were there for the show. To watch her get eaten. They had their phones out, recording. A flash of anger hit her.

She pulled the flashlight out of her jacket pocket and turned it to high beam. She hit the charging beast in the eyes with its full force. Blinded and screaming, it nevertheless kept coming.

Kirian dove out of the way and scrambled toward the room that contained the last file.

At the doorway, she drew her sleep ray gun and fired at the other guards while she was on the move. Two of the non-reptilian guards fell. She entered the records room and slammed the door, breathing heavily.

RWE010XS.

Kirian was entirely focused now. She and her flashlight were one, scanning the room. She figured the guards would help their friends and the angry reptilian; and then call for backup.

She had at least a few minutes. The first part of the new plan was to get the file. The second part was to find another way out of the room without having to go through the main area. She had lost the element of surprise.

A-ha! There it is!

RWE010XS.

Now her watch was flashing an ominous yellow warning message: "Documents due, documents due."

She uploaded the file quickly and hit 'Transmit.' The light

stopped flashing. She let out a small sigh of relief. Mission complete, all she had to do was figure out a way to get out of records alive.

She searched the room. There were no other doors, and no other windows. She was trapped. It was just going to be that kind of a day. There was a knock on the door.

"Um, occupied." Kirian didn't want them to come in, of course, but playing along with whatever delusion people offered was part of the game. And sometimes part of the fun. The door opened. It was the reptilian again, angry and ready for another shot at her. And this time it was wearing sunglasses.

"I said occupied," Kirian snapped. The effects of the flashlight had worn off faster than she hoped. Now she was trapped.

There were more security guards, and they started to chant. Not good.

Kirian pointed her flashlight, but didn't turn it on. Blast. The sunglasses were an excellent idea.

Reptilians needed almost no light to see. It could easily kill her wearing sunglasses inside. And look really cool doing it.

The security people started laughing. They had their cameras out again. Not only was Kirian going to die, but she was also going to be eaten live on camera.

She got an idea. She took a step toward the reptilian creature, stood up straight, and taunted it with the two pinkie-finger salute. The guards gasped. Could Kirian get it to make the same mistake twice? It might work. She already knew from their first encounter that the reptilian had trouble changing directions once it got going.

The reptilian charged again, mouth agape. The dripping saliva caught Kirian's attention. She watched it, mesmerized, nearly missing her chance to jump out of the way.

Once Kirian darted to the side, as she suspected, the reptilian didn't have the time or the ability to adjust its course. It slammed into the ladder teeth first.

Huh, Kirian thought, *it was dumb enough to get tricked into the same attack twice with the same result.*

The reptilian teetered for a moment, then fell to the side. Kirian knew it wouldn't stay down for long. She decided it was a good time to deal with the rest of the security guards. She sent half a dozen sleep ray blasts at the doorway leading out of the room. Some of the security guards fell. Others scattered.

"I hope you got all that on video," Kirian said, taunting the guards that were still standing. She kept firing until the room had cleared.

Something else caught Kirian's eye. One of the security guards she had blasted with the sleep ray was wearing a gothic dragon necklace on a chain around his neck. Staring at it, she was sure she had seen the symbol somewhere before.

Kirian blinked and became aware again. She felt wet and looked down. Her hands were bloody, and she was standing over the guard with the dragon necklace. She checked herself, but she had no injuries, the blood must be from the security guard.

She leaned down and checked him for a pulse. He was breathing.

Kirian, what have you done?

It must have had something to do with the dragon necklace. She took the shiny object and stuffed it into her pocket.

Whatever this was, it was an escalation of her blackouts, and it wasn't good. The security guards that had escaped were bound to come back with reinforcements.

Behind her, there was a stir. It was the reptilian again, under the ladder, shaking off the cobwebs. Kirian was out of time. She hopped over the security guards on her way out of the records department. She still had to get Ari.

Wherever you are, Ari, it's time to go.

* * *

Ari left her boss's office, clutching the papers. She wandered over to the coffee and filled her cup. Then she thought about the files that she had brought aboard Kirian's ship when she left her other planet. She considered her old boss's face as he had fired and threatened her. Finding serious problems had never gotten her anywhere good in the past. It was not how she wanted to start her new job here. Especially not on her first day with a great boss. She wanted to be able to show off, but not alarm everybody.

Hmm.

Once again, she stared out over the city through the large glass windows. Except she was here with Kirian. Would Kirian, or whoever she worked for destroy this place? It wasn't beautiful, exactly. It was, in fact, just a city, with beings running around going to jobs and family. Like every other city.

Why was there a Celestial army in the first place and why would they go around surreptitiously destroying planets? It wasn't Ari's current problem, of course, but it was there in the back of her mind. If the Octopus Overlord of the Galaxy was behind all of this, then she should indeed be held accountable.

Then again, one mystery at a time. She triple checked the results while tapping the eraser end of the pencil on the desk.

Then she made up her mind. Having no choice left, she trudged back to her new boss's office and paused outside the doorway. Then she knocked, entered and sat.

He was sitting at his desk playing some tablet game. "Well?" he asked. "Have you triple checked the numbers yet?"

Ari patiently let him finish and look up. "Yes," she answered, taking a deep breath.

Was he going to be mad? Argue with her? Try to talk her out of it? She wanted more than anything for things to stay the way they were, but she had reached a conclusion. Now it was out of her hands. "I'm afraid we're going to have to open an Intergalactic Inquiry."

His eyes grew wide. He dropped the tablet on the desk and gripped the edge of his chair. "Are you sure? I mean, are you certain that there is no other way?"

Ari exhaled. "Afraid so."

"Yes," he said, banging a fist on the desk. "I've always wanted to do that. I suspected it might be necessary myself, mind you. But I'm management, and the politicians in charge never listen to me. It's always, 'get a specialist in here and we'll listen to them.'"

He leaned forward. "If it's not too much trouble, can I see the report before you send it out?"

"Of course," Ari answered, pleasantly surprised at how the whole thing was going.

"And how soon will that be, do you think? I don't want to make you feel rushed or anything, but time is of the essence here. I want to beat everybody to the punch, you see. Maybe we're not the only ones who have figured it out."

Ari breathed a huge sigh of relief. "I'll go work on it right now. I'm not sure. If I can't get it done by this afternoon, then for certain tomorrow morning. Is that okay?"

"Splendid, my dear. Splendid." He leaned in toward her over the desk conspiratorially, which he could do because he was so spindly and tall. The effect was disconcerting.

"When you're done with that, I have another secret to tell you," he said. "Something you're going to be amazed at. Oh, it's good. You simply won't believe it. And then you will. Because it makes perfect mathematic sense, and you're the sort who appreciates those types of revelations, am I right?"

"You are right," said Ari, “and I do like a good secret.” She went to work on the Intergalactic Inquiry.

* * *

DREXYL APPROACHED the Neon Octopus Overlord after breakfast. That was when she was usually in a good mood.

His fingers clenched the coffee mug in his hand even tighter than he meant to. He hadn't slept very well. The television was on nearly twenty-four/seven now, and he suspected she was keeping an eye out for more messages between the Staars.

He hoped that in real life, the Staar bounty hunters were not as bad as they were portrayed in movies. Portable Staars, traveling between worlds wreaking malevolent destruction at will. His skin turned cold recalling late nights as a teen scaring himself watching the "true-tale" videos.

He wanted to ask Soda if she had thought the whole thing through and had a plan to save him. Because all of this was her fault, after all.

“So, how does this whole thing work? I mean with portable staar bounty hunters looking for you and all?" he asked. He tried to appear more conversational than worried.

Soda turned from the television to face him. "You want to know what I did."

He had to admit he was curious, but it wasn't his most pressing question. "I really want to know what you're going to do now that you know they're on to you."

"You worry needlessly, my boy," she said, but a bead of sweat made its way down the side of her bulbous head. "A stray message or two in a dead-end galaxy does not an emergency make."

Easy for you to say.

"I don't have to read your mind to feel your fear." She glanced at the television. "I mean, yes, they're scary and yes I'd like to avoid them, but you're underestimating my power. And my Celestials as well. Soon there will be no Palladium in this galaxy and that means no more messages. They'll just keep looking elsewhere. Forever. The universe is a really big place. Or who knows?

Maybe the staars will eventually find me. You know, Drexyl, it's uncertainty that makes the world go around."

Drexyl was pretty sure it wasn't uncertainty that made the world go around. He guessed it was money. Either way, he was probably screwed.

"Fine. We'll continue this conversation later when you're in a better mood," she cooed. "Now where are we with the planetary reports?"

"Most of them are in. Waiting on a few."

"Which few?"

"Jadnl, Keeemncs, Reptar, Iuipper..." *Reptar,* he thought. *Oh boy, that's where Kirian is.* He didn't mention it because it might set Soda off again.

He continued talking in an attempt to distract Soda from Reptar. "I mean, you have all of the power and resources of the galaxy and you just hang around here directing an astonishingly well-funded campaign to arbitrarily destroy planets. It doesn't make any sense. If I were you, I'd be out partying, for sure."

"It's not arbitrary." Soda's voice was icy.

Drexyl froze.

"I'm the oldest being in this Galaxy. I'm the smartest, most efficient being there is. That's why I was appointed Overlord. I make all the decisions, and things move happily along. And I've never received a single complaint." She finished with a flourish of waving tentacles.

"Not since you changed the rules saying you can't complain on behalf of someone else." Drexyl chimed in.

"Makes perfect sense," said Soda. "The board agreed immediately."

Because dead people can't complain.

"What did you think?" Soda demanded.

Soda couldn't read his thoughts, exactly. It took an aggregate amount of info on context, speech patterns, body language and physical sensors in her tentacles to guess. Soda was very good at guessing.

"Nothing."

A noise blared, and a blinking yellow button shone on the far end of the console. Soda hit the button, the alarm stopped, and a message appeared on the screen.

"What is it?" he asked. "What's going on?"

Drexyl saw all of Soda's tentacles deflate. What was going on?

Her face sucked itself in until Drexyl thought she would swallow her beak. An angry scream filled the room and tentacles lashed out, breaking nearby cups and knickknacks.

Drexyl ducked down, hoping to stay out of the way of any collateral damage. He waited for the wave of noise and movement to subside, but a tentacle, sharp and pointy with anger, lashed out and cut his right calf.

Blood ran down his leg. Not a lot, but the whole outburst was surprising. Soda quivered in the corner. With rage, Drexyl guessed.

He took a step toward the console and started reading.

"Official notice of Intergalactic Inquiry." He turned to Soda. "Well that's not so bad, is it? I mean, at least it's not an official complaint, right?"

Whatever caused the outburst, Drexyl was committed to making sure it didn't happen again. He had to calm Soda down. A quick glance in her direction revealed that had not yet happened.

"From where, exactly," she asked, her voice quivering, "did the Intergalactic Inquiry Originate?"

Drexyl turned back to the screen and scanned the message. *Stars. No. It can't be. Please, no.*

"Where, Drexyl?" A tentacle flew across the room. Instead of his ankle, this time it grabbed his throat. It squeezed. Not enough to kill him, not even sufficient to keep him from talking. Just exactly enough to make Drexyl think about life and death.

"Reptar," he wheezed.

* * *

AFTER A VERY SATISFYING lunch downtown with her new boss and co-workers, Ari settled at her desk to work on the Intergalactic Inquiry.

She made copies of everything she could find. Hard copies, which she printed out, bound and stuffed into locked drawers in her brand-new office. She made digital files as well and beamed them back to Fleek's ship.

She created a new folder in an entertainment drive and called it "hub files." The boring folder name paired with the unlikely event that anybody would ever look for something important buried in a space ship's entertainment drive made her feel much better. The information was secure.

All of that done, she could finally get down to the actual work of the Intergalactic Inquiry itself. This was big. The kind of thing that put an entire planet on the map big. Now Ari understood why her new boss wanted a second opinion before proceeding. One does not want to be the person responsible for bringing unprecedented attention from galactic-level governmental authorities and make a mistake.

Ari scrutinized every detail and went over every concept. It was still just an Inquiry, not an actual complaint. Not yet, anyway. There was no question in Ari's mind that there was enough information for a complaint, but there were procedures in place. Ari assumed that they were there for a reason, and she was prepared to respect them.

She finished the form and triple checked it. It was fine. She should have just taken it to her boss, but she wasn't quite ready. She backed up the actual form the same way she had backed up the other information. It left all her saved paperwork in a neat little bow. She liked neat little bows.

She carried a copy of the finished paperwork across the hall and presented it to her boss. "Here you go. Feel free to check it yourself, but believe me, it's perfect."

His face beamed as he skimmed one page and then the next. "Well done, Ari, well done. I knew you could do it." He looked up at her and smiled. "Of course, I suspected it as well; it's just that nobody believed me. And I couldn't prove it. And now here I am, staring at it in black and white."

He smiled again. This time it bothered Ari a little. Partially because his mouth was more round than wide and when he tried to go wider with it, well it just looked hideous. And partially because in his hand was a laser gun that was pointed at her head.

"Surprised?" he asked. "I knew you would be. Isn't this a great secret? I'm going to file it myself."

Ari slumped into her chair. *Not again. Why do all of my bosses turn out to be jerks?*

She should have known her first day on the job was going way too well. Kirian would probably throw this right back in her face.

Oh yeah, Kirian.

"You're making a big mistake," she told him, raising her hands. "I'm not here alone. I'm with a Celestial."

"That's the worst lie I've ever heard. Celestials are just a space myth. Like Seahorses."

Despite the threatening gesture with the gun, if he was in a hurry to kill her it didn't show. Maybe she could use this to stall. She was here with Kirian, and with any luck, she would show up in time to save her. Again.

"It's true, believe it or not." Ari leaned forward enough to whisper conspiratorially, but hopefully not enough to make him shoot her. "I'm here with Kirian, Destroyer of Planets."

Stars, Kirian was right, it was a pretty great title. For a moment, the certainty in her boss's face faltered.

"I doubt it," he said. "But hey, I've got some time. I'm going to look this Inquiry over. We'll wait for this Planet Destroyer of yours together."

He looked down, shuffled a few of the pages, and then looked up again.

"Just in case, though, I'll call security and tell them to round up all of the new hires and any unidentified persons acting suspiciously. Security just loves blanket excuses to round people up. Your friend, if she isn't imaginary, is about to be captured." He picked up the phone and dialed.

Ari swallowed. *Sorry, Kirian.*

Chapter 11

Spika pulled his brand new, specially made, heat resistant boots up on the console in full view of the handful of prisoners in the holding cell behind him.

"Cobalt blue, the last pair in my size. I've been waiting eons for these babies. What do you guys think?" It was very hard, as a staar to find stylish, mega heat resistant clothing.

"Hot!" a prisoner in the back of the ship yelled.

"What are you talking about? It's only," he checked the space ship's temperature gauge, "a hundred and five degrees. It's down several degrees since last time, bunch of whiners. There's plenty of water back there." It was irritating that they didn't appreciate his new boots.

He shook his head. Prisoners these days were so self-centered. They just weren't as conversational as in ages gone by. Back then you had your real bad guys, beings who could talk your ear off. Sometimes the bad guys could almost get you to set them free, even. It had nearly happened more than once.

Then, he would drop the prisoners off at the correctional facility, after exchanging contact information- for taunting purposes, of course. What good was a nemesis if you didn't keep in touch?

At a later time, if he was really lucky, his nemesis would escape. Then the chase was on. Information gained from each other during hours or days of back and forth during interstellar travel would be used in the search. It always made the reunions epic, with one-liners and name calling. Those were the days he missed the most. Now all he got were intermittent complaints about being hot. *Lame*.

A beep told him the ship was approaching the correctional facility.

"You know," he said, "for a bunch of small time, garden variety criminals, you sure are complainers. I remember the Ice Marlin bounty hunters in the Sardoff system eons ago. Kept their ship at twenty below. Only ten percent of them ever reached the jail alive. And I'll bet they complained less than you guys."

He landed the craft, then went to the door to check the identification of the guards who had come for the prisoners. Standard and boring procedure. Here are the prisoners. Sign the documents.

Spika paused before hitting the button to resume flight. Where to? And what was the point, exactly? Were there any real villains left in the universe?

Real villains. If only. There was the Intergalactic hot list, of course, no pun intended. A dozen or so of the worst villains at any given time who had committed serious enough violations to be chased across galaxies. Of course, villains with the intelligence and ability to escape the galaxy were few and far between in the first place. And it would take a being of infinite patience to pursue them into endless space. Infinite patience, lots of research and a wormhole full of luck.

Spika considered himself a patient Staar. He had waited a long time for the new boots. He admired their shiny-ness as well as the hard-core buckles. Some things were worth the wait.

But his patience and research budget weren't endless. So, he had set very specifically, thoroughly-researched probability traps into the void hoping one of them would be triggered. It was a very, very, very long shot. Sort of like the odds of catching a fish by blindly throwing a spear into a river that had a small population of fish.

He tapped into the console to check on the traps. One of them had, in fact, been triggered. He pulled out his phone. Oh yes, there it is.

He frowned. The notification had been sent to him decades ago, but the phone had been on mute. He checked, but there were no additional messages.

Maybe he should get out more. Meet people. Do the fun stuff he saw on television. He thought about it and decided it was a bad idea. Television existed so he could experience all of those things without having to encounter other beings on their turf, endure their mindless banalities, and laugh at their stupid jokes.

Cheers to you, television.

Television and take-out food. The two best inventions in the history of the universe.

Okay, back to the trap.

Step one, wait for a trigger. Step two, send out a warning. He tapped in the standard intergalactic "we're coming for you" tripe.

Done.

The message was transmitted to everything within twenty light years of the trigger. The actual triangulation of the calculations necessary to narrow down the quadrant for the trigger would take a while to calculate. So, he set the program running on the computer and then turned his mind to more pressing matters. Take-out food. Pizza or burgers? Maybe BBQ.

The alarm had been triggered, and that was something to celebrate. Tonight, it would be steak. Steak take-out was tricky, though, and would take a lot of sifting through restaurant reviews.

While he ate, Spika glanced at the area still triangulating on the console map.

Huh, that's weird.

A massive area within the triangulation was running dangerously low on Palladium. Maybe he should send out a tracer. He hadn't sent out a tracer in years. The thought excited him. The old cat and mouse game.

The tracer process was both a secret and a long shot. Less than three percent of tracers hit a target. It only worked on living Palladium. If it did hit a target though, it boosted the Palladium level in the whole area.

Of course, he could never enter that type of command into the console if prisoners were watching. They couldn't know the secrets of the Staars. But he had just dropped them all off; the place was empty. Just him and dinner.

He decided to go for it. Another job buzzed in, but he ignored it for now. He deployed the tracer. Then, with a feeling of satisfaction, he sat back. Maybe his luck was finally turning.

Chapter 12

Kirian made her way toward the office where she'd left Ari. It was obvious that she had been made, security was everywhere now, searching for her.

She exited the elevator, ran down the hallway, and approached the executive level. She ducked into Ari's office. Nobody was home.

She searched room to room, kicking open doors along the hallway looking for her. She'd have been more polite about it, but this planet was pissing her off. A different alarm went off on her watch. Not again. An electric shock pulsed through her bracelets. Dropping to her knees, she screamed.

"Kirian?" It was Ari's voice.

The electric buzzing stopped. Kirian got up unsteadily and ducked her head into the office Ari's voice had come from. Ari was sitting in a chair, and her boss was behind the desk. The boss had a gun out, and it was trained on Ari. The minute Kirian stepped into the doorway; the gun pointed at her instead.

"Hello, Ari," Kirian announced, unfazed by the gun. "I haven't checked the deletion data yet for this planet, but I'm assuming you've changed your mind about staying, yes?"

"Thanks for not throwing that in my face," Ari answered. "I appreciate it."

"What's going on?" New Boss got tired of being ignored.

"Told you," Ari said triumphantly. "Meet Kirian, Destroyer of Planets."

Ari glanced at Kirian behind her. "Kirian, what happened? Are you okay?"

That's when Kirian remembered that her clothes were covered in blood, but there was nothing she could do about that now.

"Look," said Kirian, taking a step toward Ari's boss. "I'm not in the mood for this. It's been a crappy day so far. Just let Ari go, and I won't hurt you." She turned to Ari. "I'm ok. The blood isn't mine."

"You're not going anywhere," New Boss answered. "Either of you." He waved the gun from one girl to the other and then back.

"Ari, what's going on here? We don't have time for this. How many of your bosses do I have to kill, anyway?"

The boss tried to look more menacing in light of these new revelations, but he was already maxed out. Kirian squinted at the gun in his hand—a Jkeasden 550, mostly decorative. It probably wasn't even fully charged.

"That's a pretty toy," Kirian said, and then dove to her left behind a water cooler. As she suspected, the gun followed her movement.

Kirian pulled out her sleep ray and fired from the cover of the water cooler. New Boss fired too, but the weak ray simply bounced off of the cooler and ricocheted into the wall, making a small popping noise. Kirian's blast hit its mark. New boss's head fell forward with a thump onto the desk.

Kirian turned in the direction of the doorway to go, but Ari was headed for her now sleeping boss. What now?

Ari unceremoniously wrenched the man's head up, grabbed the papers underneath, then let go again. His head fell hard and made a loud, hollow thud that echoed around the room. Then she kicked him in the shin.

Atta girl. "Feel better now, Ari? Let's go."

"One more minute." Ari darted in Kirian's direction, which was good, then back toward her office, which was decidedly bad.

"We're out of minutes, Ari. Security is all over the place looking for me."

She waited for a sign that Ari understood what a hurry they were in.

"Ari, are you listening?"

Ari tapped furiously on her keypad. "Done," Ari announced.

"Look," said Kirian, "what was so important that you continued to put both of our lives in danger despite me telling you that we absolutely, positively had to leave?" The answer had better be good, or she would save Ari only to drop her off at the equivalent of the first interstellar truck stop they happened to come across. She clenched her fists.

Ari was up from behind the desk and running towards her now. "Sorry. I had to file an official Intergalactic Inquiry."

"You did what?" Kirian asked, but as soon as the words left her mouth, she found it impossible to focus.

"Aren't we supposed to be leaving?" Ari asked. "Kirian. You okay?"

Kirian swayed and started deep breathing. "Do you have any idea what you've done?"

"The Inquiry? Oh, believe me, nothing to fear. All my ducks were in a row. I kept copies of everything and—"

An alarm started blaring overhead accompanied by menacing red flashing lights. Kirian gulped in some air, grabbed Ari, and ran.

* * *

"REPTAR," Soda repeated. "Isn't that where your girlfriend is? That

Kirian?"

Soda concentrated on Kirian. It made her slightly dizzy, but sent electric shocks into Kirian's handcuffs. It was the only thing she could think to do in her rage.

"Do you know what this means?" she quaked. "Meetings. Formal interviews. You have no idea what it's like. These board members are so stupid and tedious."

Soda took a breath and attempted to stop shaking.

Drexyl was still suspended in the air by his neck, hanging from a trembling tentacle. Soda blinked and released him. He fell and landed with a thud which, ironically, seemed to knock the wind back into him.

"Sorry. And you're welcome."

"That's you," coughed Drexyl. "Always coming to my rescue after you nearly kill me."

She watched him gulp in air.

"Why do you care?" he asked. "What does a single complaint even matter? In fact, let me point out that it is not even a complaint, it's just an inquiry."

"What does it matter?" The anger was causing purple spots in her vision now. She laid down all of her tentacles and tried to assume a relaxed posture like it said to do in the Ancient and Special Species Relaxation Manual she had just spent oodles of money on. So far it had not worked as advertised.

"It matters," Soda said, inhaling in through her nose and out through her beak, as per the book's instructions. Unlike most of the advice, the structured breathing was starting to help.

"Because now they have a way into my world, my life, my time. I was insulated by the lack of complaints. I know all of this because I wrote my contract. And now it's only a matter of time before—"

The console emitted a beep. Drexyl hit a button to answer the communication.

"Take a message," she ordered.

"Um," said Drexyl. "Her Supreme Overlord, Highness of the Galaxy can't come to the communicator right now." He turned to stare at her before continuing. "Can I take a message?"

"The Intergalactic Civilian Oversight Committee requests your presence immediately for an informal question and answer session regarding a recently received Inquiry."

"Great," deadpanned Soda, "just perfect. Now I have to find my formal jeans."

* * *

KIRIAN LED Ari out of the labyrinthine building, using her watch to navigate.

"Why are we hurrying so much? Is the planet going to be deleted or not?"

Kirian realized that she hadn't checked. "Because security is looking for us. Let's get out of the building first, or would you like to spend the last few moments of your life in a prison cell?"

They exited the skyscraper into daylight and ducked down an alley. Kirian checked her communicator, fully expecting a planetary deletion order but she was wrong. She checked again.

"Weird."

"What?"

"It's a green light. The planet won't be destroyed. There hasn't been a green light in quite a while."

"This stupid planet gets to live?"

"I'm as unhappy about that as you, Ari. But hey, those are the breaks."

A large, green, heavily-muscled creature stepped into the alley with them and put a gun to Kirian's temple.

"Hello, Kirian. We gotta stop meeting this way." He looked Kirian over. "You look even worse than usual."

"Ari," said Kirian, "meet Kracken. He's been trying to kill me for the last three dozen missions."

Chapter 13

"How's the research going, Trish? Nothing like waiting until the last minute."

Trisha started and closed her laptop. "You can't just sneak up on people like that."

Jen smirked and continued to lurk in Trisha's dorm doorway. "You look like you just saw a ghost. What topic did you get stuck with, anyway?"

Jen was right, though. Trisha waited too long to choose a thesis topic, and all the good ones had already been taken, so she was stuck sifting through the butt end of the dark net investigating conspiracy theories. To graduate, each of the seventy-three members of the senior class of the Benadign University of Journalism had to study conspiracy theories.

In fact, hers was one of the last classes to do so, if she were graduating just two years later, she'd be able to investigate something normal, like local politicians or criminals or something useful.

"Trish?"

"Oh, yeah. I'm investigating Celestial. Crazy stuff. It's the weirdest of online conspiracy theories about secret government projects, brainwashing, and planetary destruction. I would give anything to have picked the mythical sea monsters on the beach planet of Grenadine. But no, now I'm having to stay up late every night scaring the stars out of myself on the dark net."

"Sounds rough. I'm already done."

"Bite me."

"You sound cranky. Wanna go get something to eat?"

Trisha checked her watch. Four a.m. There was no way she was getting to sleep anytime soon with all of the stuff she had just read. "I'm game if you are. If you're already done with your thesis, then why are you up this late?"

"Gaming. Just got killed. I have to go blow off some steam. Hang on, let me grab my purse."

Trisha followed Jen to her room. The television showed a neon blue octopus. Trisha ducked in to read the text at the bottom of the screen since the volume was turned down.

The text said: *First ever board meeting with the Galactic Octopus Overseer to happen soon in Arcturis City.*

"I've got my purse," Jen announced.

"Hey," said Trisha, pointing at the tv, "have you seen this news story about the Neon Octopus Overlord? Fascinating. I'd love to meet her."

Trisha pointed at the screen and thought about how very little ever happened in this town and how cool it would be to get to interview the famous and powerful people. "Is this meeting open to the public? Just one official rebuttal by her would give me enough points to finish my thesis early."

"Yeah, right," Jen answered. "No way they're letting you within a light year of that meeting. You ready to go eat?"

"I'm ready," Tricia answered. This was the reason she had gotten into journalism in the first place. To fight for answers. To confront the rich and powerful and all of that stuff. Plus, she was overdue for some shopping in the capital. She knew that the possibility of meeting the Overseer, even for a moment, was worth fighting for.

Chapter 14

"Not kill you, darling," Kracken said, "just stop you. You Celestials need to be stopped. I'm still holding out hope that we can turn you to our side."

"No thanks. No conspiracy crackpots for me." Kirian risked raising one hand and twirled a finger near her ear, making the intergalactic sign of crazy for Ari's benefit.

"How is this anti-Celestial guy a crackpot?" Ari butted in, unable to help it. "You're literally right here. Right now. Checking to see if this planet is going to be deleted."

"Ari, is it?" Kracken asked, still not lowering the gun.

Ari studied Kracken. When he turned his head, she thought she might have seen gills. And he was easy on the eyes. "Yes, nice to meet you. And by the way, she said the planet's not going to be deleted."

"No?" Kracken sounded disappointed.

"See?" Kirian said to Ari. "Crazy."

"Alright then," said Kracken, "I guess we'll just fast forward to standard procedures, then."

"What are the standard procedures?" Ari asked.

"Getting plastered at the nearest pub," Kirian answered.

"I thought we were in a terrible hurry," Ari countered. "And he just had a gun to your head."

"Well, I turned in my paperwork, and for once the planet's not going to be destroyed. Besides, not my choice," replied Kirian, pointing to Kracken. "Gun to my head and all. Am I right, Kracken?"

"True that, missy." He put his gun in his pocket and led the way. "And don't you go running off or I'll kill you deader than a sand flea on Bora Tora in the Garb system and—"

"She gets the point, Kracken."

* * *

"So Kirian," said Kracken as they sat at a bar down the street, "what in the stars re-aligning allowed you to make a friend?"

He looked appraisingly at Ari.

Kirian laughed. "Ari's great. You're going to like her."

"Oh, I already do," he said, throwing his head back and downing an enormous foamy beverage.

Ari watched him. Kracken was tall, as tall as Kirian. He did have gills, and he gave off a pirate-y vibe. He also had a mischievous grin that made him handsome in a roguish way. Ari decided she liked him. He winked at her.

"So, you guys are basically just drinking buddies?" Ari looked from Kirian to Kracken. "What is it that you do, exactly, Kracken?"

"Well," he said, giving a quick nod to the bartender, who refilled his glass, confirming to Ari that he was nobody to be trifled with. Her small glass had been empty for the last couple of minutes with no refill in sight. "I follow her around and try to get in her way a little. See if I can't save a planet or two from Kirian-Destroyer of Planets."

That made Kirian laugh again. "Hey Ari, does that sound familiar?"

Kirian's drink was blue, and also on fire.

"Did you ever succeed?" Ari asked. "At saving any planets?"

"No, love. Not yet."

"I don't understand. Then why do it in the first place? Especially since you've never been successful?"

"Success doesn't always mean victory, love," Kracken said.

Ari watched him finish off another giant glass. She frowned at him, how could he drink that much? What was he made of? And Kirian seemed to be keeping pace.

"And it's not Kirian or the other Celestials that we are really trying to stop," Kracken continued, "it's that Octopus Overseer in charge of the Galaxy. We're pretty sure the conspiracy goes all the way to the top. Nobody else could get away with it. And I'm the one who gets to shadow Kirian because I'm the best."

Ari swallowed hard. As far as she knew, that was where the Official Intergalactic Inquiries end up. At the top. With the Overseer.

In her defense, Ari was merely using the correct channels to properly report a question or concern in the form of an Inquiry. Something that any brilliant and concerned citizen should do under the circumstances, but the possibilities hit her all at once. If the Overseer was doing illegal or improper things on purpose, then calling attention to it could be bad.

"Oh yeah," Kirian said, putting her empty glass down with emphasis, "that reminds me. And you are going to love this Kracken. Ari, tell him what you did today. I mean, it'll probably get me killed, but in some ways, for the galaxy, I guess it's progress."

Kracken put down the glass and turned his full attention to Ari. "What is Kirian going on about, then?"

"Um," said Ari and looked at Kirian. Kirian didn't help at all, she simply lifted her eyebrows a little in anticipation.

A wave of uneasiness and regret washed over Ari. She didn't want to get anyone killed, much less Kirian, who had saved her life. Twice. And now she knew that Kirian was only doing what she had to do as a prisoner herself.

"Um, I filed a report today."

"Wait for it," said Kirian, and gave Ari a get-on-with-it look.

Ari decided it was best to just blurt it out. Plus, her tiny drink was starting to kick in. "I filed an Official Intergalactic Inquiry."

Kracken's eyes got wide. "You did what?"

He clapped his hands together, stood up, and started dancing. He was surprisingly good. He caught the bartender's attention again with barely a wave. "Another round," he said, indicating the three of them, and then thought better of it. "In fact, drinks for everybody. On me!"

The few dozen patrons roared in approval.

Kracken caught Ari by the hand and pulled her onto the dance floor. Ari was nowhere near drunk enough for this type of thing, but he was very charming and persuasive.

"Why are you so happy about the report?" Ari asked.

He kept dancing and whirled her around, ignoring her question.

"Pardon me, love, but you don't seem the kind of person who would file a ground-breaking Intergalactic Overseer-antagonizing form without dotting the 'I's and crossing the 'T's and making sure you have the proper standing and all that sort of thing, am I right?"

Ari stopped dancing. "I don't know what you're implying, but I had absolute proper standing and raised significant and acceptable questions in an accurate and legal way."

Kracken stopped dancing too. An alarming, vicious smile crawled across his face. He exchanged glances with Kirian. Then he turned back to Ari and leaned in. "Good. Now that's what I'm talking about. Why is it that you have no idea what you've just done?"

"I found significant mathematical anomalies where none

should exist. I did something about it. I filed a form. I don't understand why it's such a big deal."

She was starting to understand, but decided denial was the way to go for now.

"What you've just done is forever alter the contract of the Overseer. Things may go really good or bad from now on, but they'll never be the same. You've punched a hole in the contract."

He began dancing again, and she played along. Thinking. The situation required a lot of thinking. The Overseer and the contract? Getting Kirian killed? Changing the Galaxy as everybody knew it? What in the name of all of the pretty stars did any of this have to do with math oddities?

"How do you know so much about the Overseer and her contract?" Ari demanded.

Kracken didn't answer.

"Wait," she said after being twirled. "That's what we're doing here, right? We're waiting for something."

"You're pretty smart, just like Kirian said."

Ari unwrapped herself from Kracken's arms, returned to the bar, and sat next to Kirian. "What exactly are we waiting for?"

"A reaction," Kirian said, smiling. Then she put her emptied glass down and wiped her face. "You asked why I saved you."

"Yes, I did."

"Well," said Kirian, looking at her black gadget watch, "I may not have saved you for very long, depending on what happens next, but I may as well tell you the honest reason. You're the smartest being I have ever come across. I thought if I lived long enough, well, maybe you could figure out a way. To help me."

"To free you. From the bracelets."

"That would be nice," Kirian replied, "but mostly, so I can kill the Overseer."

Ari looked at Kracken, who had followed her back to eavesdrop. "The other reason you're not mad at her. You're using her."

Kracken shrugged.

"Well," said Ari, "for my part, I'm sorry. I wasn't trying to make your life more difficult, Kirian."

It was nearly impossible to wrap her head around. A being as powerful as Kirian being held prisoner. Especially with the fancy ship and the money and the whole idea of Celestial itself being so preposterous.

"So, what are we really waiting for here, then?" Ari asked.

"For a response. I told you. My boss, the Overseer, is very passive-aggressive. And she doesn't know you're here. You're supposed to be dead, remember? I assume the rest of the people on this planet are idiots. I always do. So, when the Overseer receives your Inquiry, who do you think she's going to blame?"

Ari finally understood. "Kirian, we should get out of here right now. Back to the ship."

At that moment, the ground began to shake. The entire bar lurched forward, toward the middle of the room, taking all of the glasses and a couple of patrons with it. At the same time, the back of the room tilted in on itself.

Then, as quickly as it began, it ended. The floor straightened back out.

"What was that?" Ari asked.

"The answer we were waiting for," Kracken answered. "It's sort of a 'good news and bad news' type of thing."

"How's that again?"

"Well," he answered, "the good news is that your little Intergalactic Inquiry thing must have gone all the way to the top. The bad news is, the Overseer's probably going to destroy this planet now. And she thinks it was Kirian who filed the report."

The bar emptied quickly. Soon only Ari, Kracken, and Kirian remained.

"Kirian's the only person on the planet who has a clue, as far as the Overseer knows."

"But it wasn't Kirian, obviously. It was me. There's no way she could have done the math for this." Ari indicated Kirian. "No offense."

"None taken," Kirian answered. "But as far as the Overseer knows, you're dead."

"The thing is," Kracken said, "I've been tracking Celestial for a long time now, love, and most of the time it's carbon-based life forms and non-precious metals that are being eradicated. What the Overseer is mostly destroying appears to be intelligence. We don't know why. It's atypical, even for a politician. That's why it's been so damn hard to figure out. Usually these things, conspiracies I mean, are just about money or power."

"And the Overseer already has both." Ari shook her head. "You're saying that the planet I was on was destroyed because of me?"

Kracken smiled at her. "If you're capable of filing an Intergalactic Inquiry that rattled the cage of the most powerful being in the galaxy, then yes. I can guarantee the planet you were on was destroyed because of you."

"Can you two wrap it up?" Kirian asked, butting in. "We should probably get back to the ship. I've seen this happen a hundred times and this planet isn't going to last much longer."

* * *

What is wrong with that Octopus?

Floyd brooded. How dare she kill the secret army he wasn't finished stealing from her yet? Floyd tried frowning, but it never worked. Not with his underlying bone structure, not even with the species-hiding avatar projection software he had pioneered. His species was strictly forbidden in this galaxy.

Time to do something about it. He closed and locked the door to his office and dialed the octopus in her lair. The pretty-boy showed up on the screen first.

"Soda, it's Floyd," Drexyl called.

"What does he want?" she yelled back. "Tell him I'm not here."

At that moment, Floyd wished he was capable of rolling his eyes. She never left the lair, she never went anywhere. If anything, she was lazier than he was, and it bothered him a lot. She was beating him at his own game.

"I know you're there," Floyd said. "This is important, uh, Soda. I'll be quick." The octopus had a lot of titles that Floyd knew of, but Soda was a new one to him.

She entered the screen and stood, uninterested, inspecting her tentacles.

"What is it, Floyd? I'm busy."

"So I see," Floyd retorted. "Hey, I read a very disturbing update on the Celestial program. Something about two more missions and then the whole thing being dissolved? That can't possibly be right."

She glared at him. "No. That's correct."

Floyd could blink, so he did. "Think about what you're throwing away here. You have to know what these Celestials are capable of. And the work I was doing with them...well, in my opinion, you should reconsider."

"What time is it, Drexyl?" she shouted to pretty-boy off screen, ignoring Floyd's advice.

"You've got six minutes until All My Nebulae starts," he shouted back.

Soda returned her attention to Floyd.

"For stars' sake, Floyd, it's sweeps week. There are still two more missions left, and the last one is in Vega of all places, which is going to be a big headache. So just do your job. And I know exactly what the Celestials can do, I built them from the ground up. And I'll rebuild them again, eventually... Drexyl, make the popcorn."

"Maybe you could extend the time line, then, for six months or so. What I'm trying to tell you here is that I'm making wonderful progress as the Head Brainwashing Coordinator. I'm way better than the last guy, and if you will just give me some more time-"

"Look, Floyd. You're great and all." Unlike Floyd, Soda could, and did, roll her eyes.

A quiver of rage trembled in his thorax. He had to fight to keep it under control. "But you're an intern. You're here to make my life easier, and right now you're not. You've got two more missions. Deal with it. Then find something else to do. When I put another round of Celestials together, I'll give you a call, okay?"

Soda shot her pretty-boy a look that Floyd was pretty sure meant she had no intention of ever calling him back. Then she hung up on him.

Floyd sat in the silence that followed. He shivered with rage. He couldn't remember the last time he'd been this angry. Now he would have to figure out a way to stop her. Ugh, actual work.

He decided to stalk and kill something; that always made him feel better. Then he'd know what to do next.

* * *

FLEEK SAT with his feet up on the bridge console. He checked his appearance in the shiny metallic finish.

Carpe sat in a chair nearby, eyeing him suspiciously. It made him nervous.

It shouldn't have made Fleek so nervous. Every detail was perfect. In every way, he looked the role of a rock star. Blond, longish Mohawk- check. Blue lipstick-check. Guy-liner-check. He smiled. The best part was that he looked nothing like the dark haired, clean cut, suit-wearing guy he had been before he faked his death. So why was this guy so suspicious?

Carpe cleared his throat. "You told me you lived with a Celestial."

"I do."

"Look, Fleek. If you were lying to me, about a single thing you said on the phone, I will gut you like a fish." Carpe pulled a large, curved blade out of his clothing with one of his four arms. The double set of arms and the fin on top of his head only added to his menacing look. "And I will take your head back to Regal to explain why I left."

Carpe quietly cursed his instincts, stars, black holes, and those little cinnamon rolls that never have enough icing.

"Patience," Fleek said.

Judging by Carpe's reaction, it was the wrong thing to say. He advanced, brandishing the curved sword.

Fleek jumped to his feet and held up his hands. "Hey, man. It's about the music, remember? Besides, every single thing I told you is one hundred percent true. Everything. I promise."

Carpe stopped advancing and stood still for a moment. He sat back down heavily. "Okay," he said. "You have ten minutes. Then I'll gut you. Unless, of course, a Celestial comes through that portal."

"Don't worry," said Fleek, although, truth be told, Carpe didn't look at all worried. Fleek was the one who was starting to worry. Kirian was way overdue. "Where was I?"

Carpe gave him a hungry, feral grin. "You were telling me not to worry."

"Right." Fleek regained a little self-control. The fractals gave him courage; the music was his strength. "Just saying though, once Kirian, Destroyer of Planets comes through that portal, you have to trust me. No more threats, no more second guessing. You'll be a member of the band. Don't get me wrong, you were chosen because of your background, and it's going to come in handy. You just can't aim it at me anymore. Got it?"

Carpe considered this. "Ok. If this Kirian proves legit, and the band is real, then fine." He looked down at his watch and shook his head. "Trust me; I'm rooting on the band. But your time's running out, mate. You only have one hundred and twenty seconds."

Fleek's heart started racing. He felt a drop of moisture work its way from his hairline down his cheek. Carpe was watching him carefully.

"Sixty seconds."

Fleek ran his fingers through his Mohawk again.

And that's when three beings fell through the portal and landed in a heap on the floor.

Fleek looked at the jumble of arms, legs, and bodies, and tried to figure out why there were three of them. He re-counted with the same result. There was Kirian, who flopped forward onto the floor. Then there was Ari. And some other guy.

"Hello, Ari."

Kirian was covered in blood.

"What's wrong with Kirian?" Fleek asked.

"It's not my blood," Kirian answered. "Fleek, fire in the hole again. Get us out of here!"

Fleek glanced at Carpe, who raised a green eyebrow back at him.

"Fire in the hole," said Fleek in response to the eyebrow raise, "try to keep up, Carpe." He sat in the pilot's chair, strapped himself in, and tapped open the controls. "That means go fast. I can do that."

"Who's he?" Ari asked Fleek, pointing to Carpe.

"Who's that?" Fleek asked about Kracken, while his fingers danced over the controls.

"Touché."

"What about my ship?" Kracken said.

"Hang your stupid ship," Ari said. "We have to get out of here now."

Fleek continued tapping at the controls. Kracken glared at Ari.

"Fine," Ari said. "You want to do this? Where did you leave your stupid ship?"

"On the planet," Kracken answered.

Ari shot him a think-about-that-for-a minute-look. She grabbed onto something and held tight.

"I like her," Carpe told Fleek, his head gesturing at Ari.

"If the rest of you would stop distracting me," Fleek said, "I'd like to keep us from blowing up."

The ship shot into warp, and everything got all fuzzy for Ari. First, her stomach did several front flips followed by half a back flip. Then it left her body completely to flit around the space ship without her.

The people around her became blurred forms. Ari didn't know exactly what was going on, but so far it wasn't so bad. At least she was hanging onto something this time instead of careening around the ship bumping into things.

Ari had a thousand different questions about the technology being employed, its effects on beings like herself, and where exactly they were going. Those questions would have to wait until whatever this was stopped, and the beings around her took their proper shape again.

There was a loud noise and a serious vibration. The ship did several actual loops. Just as well that her stomach was having an out of body experience.

The ship's new antics threw all of them around the cabin, except for Fleek who was strapped in. It was quite like the scenario she was worried about to begin with.

Up became down, and then up again, and then the lights went out. Ari hit the floor and the ceiling in succession several times. There were screams and groans all around her.

After what felt like an eternity, but was probably only a few seconds, several things happened.

The ship stopped flipping.

Yay.

Then the lights came back on.

Everybody was scattered around on what was, in fact, the ceiling. It took Ari a moment to figure out exactly why everything looked different.

The last thing Ari saw before the ship flipped itself again was everybody other than herself grab onto something. The result was Ari hitting the ship's floor hard, again, on her back. It knocked the breath out of her body.

Ari lay there gasping. She gave her stomach a moment to return to her, but it stubbornly refused.

Fleek unbuckled from the pilot's chair looking unruffled. He spun around to face Ari. "Hey, what happened to Kirian?"

"This is your Celestial?" The new guy had a thick muscular frame displaying colorful tattoos that at first glance looked both ocean-themed and highly inappropriate.

Fleek motioned to Kirian. "Carpe," he said ceremoniously, "meet Kirian, Destroyer of Planets."

Kirian stood and faced him in her blood-soaked clothes. "Sorry to disappoint. You were expecting what?"

"I guess that looks about right." He still seemed unsure, though.

"I'm sorry, who are you and what are you doing here?" Ari asked.

Fleek's face drained of color. "Says the girl who's been on the ship for like two days? Did I say that to you when Kirian brought you on board? Did I give you the third degree? No, I said, hello Ari, nice to meet you. Because some people on this ship have manners."

Ari was surprised. She didn't see Fleek's outburst coming. She had manners, but the new guy looked scary, and he was questioning Kirian. She looked from Carpe to Kracken, though, and realized that the ship was filling with beings that would cause her to both lock her door and sleep with weapons from now on.

"My name's Carpe," New Guy said. "I'm the bass player."

"Bass player, sure," Ari said and turned back to Fleek.

The other thought floating around in her head was that Fleek had just saved all of their lives. If that whole fuzziness thing was warp speed or light speed or whatever, and the ship was still affected by the blast that destroyed the planet, then in orbit they wouldn't have had a chance.

Kracken slumped in the corner sulking, presumably over his lost ship. What did he think was going to happen? He should be happy to be alive.

Chapter 15

Trisha paced the threadbare carpet waiting to see if she'd get a chance to ask the Overseer her question, but her hope was fading fast.

All reporters wanting to cover the event had been cheerfully escorted into this room. Once inside, the armed guards made it clear that the press was not going to get access.

She'd probably wasted a very expensive trip, and her credit cards were already maxed out.

To make matters worse, security had thrown all of the journalists in the same room with the conspiracy theory crazies.

She slumped to the floor thinking about all of the extra research she would have to do when she got home. She'd have to pull so many all-nighters. She should have at least brought her laptop with her, to use the time to catch up on real work.

A young hipster guy with an ironic Planet Reconstruction Band t-shirt slumped down next to her. "Doesn't matter," he said, "they'll never ask her any real questions anyway."

Trisha realized he was talking to her, but he wasn't looking at her. She turned to him. "What?"

When she looked right at him his eyes bugged out a little, as though she had violated some sort of crazy conspiracy theory protocol or something.

"Don't look right at me," he hissed. "Don't you know they're always recording? What are you, crazy or something?"

Sure. I'm the crazy one. "Okay, what kind of questions *should* they be asking her?" She pretended to look down at her phone.

"Well, they should be asking her about all the disappearing planets, you know? And about her secret army. And how she's really another species in disguise."

Trisha looked up from her phone. She couldn't help it. "You don't think she's really an octopus? Then what in stars do you think she is? I mean, you've seen her on television, right?"

"Since when is television reality? Name's Brad by the way." He thrust out a hand.

She wavered back and forth about whether to give him her real name, then gave in and shook his hand. "Trisha." *If I start having to make up names for every nut case I meet, I'll get little else done.*

She snapped her notebook shut and placed it on the floor next to her. "Well, Brad," she began, "you see there's fictional television which are shows written by beings for entertainment- and those are made up, and then there are things happening in the real world and people like journalists show them to you and that's called non-fiction."

Brad laughed out loud. "You don't really believe that, do you?"

"Do you really believe that the Octopus Overseer isn't really an octopus?"

"Maybe," he said.

Trisha glanced at him. He was cute in a cocky kind of way, but she wasn't here to stoke the fires of conspiracy, she was here to cut corners on her thesis. "And just for the sake of asking, what was that bit about the disappearing planets?"

"She has this secret army she uses to destroy entire planets.

Gone in a flash. Poof." He made a puffing motion with his mouth and spread the fingers of his right hand.

"You mean the Celestials, right?"

Brad's mouth hung open and he turned to stare at her. "You know about the Celestials? You've been holding out on me." He frowned. "You're a spy, aren't you?"

"I'm not a spy, Brad. And I can prove it to you."

A wicked, ambitious idea came to her. It wasn't very nice. Not for Brad, anyway, but it would help her with her thesis, maybe. And he would simply be doing what he came here to do which was challenge authority and stir up trouble. She sat up and faced him.

"How?" he asked.

"I'm actually a journalism student. And I'm here to confront the Overseer and ask her about the Celestials. I'm studying them for my thesis, you see. But I'm going to need your help."

He nodded cautiously, but she was clearly drawing him in. "What can I do?"

"It's not going to be easy," she said with a twinge of guilt. "And you can say no," she added, hoping it would absolve her of any responsibility moving forward. "I need you to create a distraction so I can get past the guards."

A stir rippled around the room as an announcement was made that the meeting was about to adjourn.

Brad frisked himself, checking his pockets, clearly excited about the proposition. "I have just the thing right here." He pulled out what looked like firecrackers. "I'd get ready if I were you."

"How'd you get those past security?" Trisha asked.

"Don't ask."

Trisha grabbed her phone and got ready to run, eyes on the guards. Brad turned away and lit his small explosives out of their view.

"One more thing," Brad said before launching himself toward the security guards.

"What's that?" Trisha asked.

"Please bail me out," he shouted as he charged the front door and the first of the firecrackers exploded.

The other journalists dove out of the way and onto the floor. Most of the security guards made a beeline for Brad. One stood in the middle of the door, blocking the exit and holding his ground.

Trisha sprinted as fast as she could. She squirted through the left side and past the guard, whose attention was fixed on Brad.

She continued down the hallway, turned right, and then headed toward the main hall. It was a good thing that she had researched the building schematics ahead of time. Maybe she wasn't such a slacker after all.

In the distance, a small, furry creature opened the main conference room door and then, suddenly, there she stood, in all her neon blue glory. The Efficient Octopus Overseer of the Galaxy.

The sight almost took Trisha's breath away. For one brief moment, she believed her plan would work. She ran toward the Overlord. For a moment, they even made eye contact. Then, four more security guards took her down from the left. Then, her breath, quite literally, was taken away as she hit the floor.

Chapter 16

A small furry posted at the entrance to the meeting room saw her coming and cleared his throat. "Her Supreme Overseer of the Galaxy," he announced.

Soda entered the room with a flourish of tentacles. "Hello, board members," she said. "Let's get this over with."

The board members stood until she wriggled into her chair at the head of the table and then they all sat.

She tapped a tentacle on the table. "Let's get to it. I'm not interested in being here all day, gentlemen, I have things to do."

A tall being with spectacles attached to his face with suckers —he had no ears—and a baggy suit spoke first. He sat two chairs away from her, and his voice grated on her nerves.

"Your Grace," he said, "as you probably already know, we called you here to discuss the Official Intergalactic Inquiry that we recently received."

"Yes? What about it?" *The trick with these mindless yes-men is to let them know you are still the boss. Otherwise they'll walk all over you.*

She got bored as he droned on and on and scanned their

thoughts, more out of habit and ability than interest. "Hey, who called me wobbly head?" she asked.

Eight of the ten of them sat up abruptly and fidgeted or adjusted their ties.

Now she was in an even worse mood. "Somebody send for coffee. I like mine with extra sugar, extra milk, and double the rum."

She scanned the boardroom to make sure some of them were scurrying with their phones to place the order. That done, she swiveled her head to face the speaker again. "Continue."

"Well," he said, "and I know that your contract states that as long as things are humming along reasonably well we aren't allowed to bother you and all, but quite honestly, we've received a number of questions over the last few centuries. And you haven't responded to any of our electronic correspondence."

"Exactly," she replied. "My contract. I'm a busy woman, and I hold up my end of the bargain, doing my job keeping the Galaxy moving along. And what I expect from you people is to do your jobs and stop pestering me."

"But some of these questions are quite important. And you're the only one who can answer them."

She slammed a tentacle on the table. "I don't believe we are here to discuss the benefits and drawbacks of my current contract. Am I correct?"

After a quick intake of breath, baggy suit looked like he lost his train of thought.

"There is also the matter of how to handle the press." The new voice was to her right.

She turned from baggy suit to see a shorter, larger being wearing a top hat. *Ridiculous. Felt in this day and age? What was he thinking?* "No press."

"I very respectfully disagree," Felt-hat said. "I believe it's very important for there to be a sense of transparency in the running of the Galaxy. In order to make the residents feel more secure."

Soda considered this. She had already thrown her tentacle on the table. How else could she get through to these people? She breathed in and out slowly and quivered slightly. Then she really enunciated, "I said no press."

He opened his mouth to argue, but she cut him off. "Technically," she said, "it's not a complaint. It's only an Inquiry. And the Transparency Act only comes into play in the case of a complaint."

She scanned the faces again. "Are we all agreed that the point of order we are here to deal with today is in fact an Official Intergalactic Inquiry and not an Official Intergalactic Complaint? Show of hands," she requested.

Every hand in the place shot toward the vaulted ceiling. Of course. As of this moment, she was holding all of the cards, which was great, because she had eight tentacles and could hold four decks at once.

"It's just that—" Top Hat started up again, only he didn't finish his sentence on account of the tentacle wrapped around his throat.

"Anybody else have any questions about press coverage?" she asked, eyebrows raised at them.

They didn't answer. They were very distracted. Distracted and weak. Distracted by their colleague who was thrashing around, banging on the table and feebly fighting against her tentacle. Strength. It's what these weasels always responded to.

She pretended to look at her fingernails, ignoring the frantic pleas of the other board members. The room became thick with fear.

But her fingernails were atrocious. She was decades overdue for a manicure. She tried to remember the name of the lady she really liked at the salon she hoped had not gone out of business in the previous thirty years.

The thought reminded her of something else. "And another thing, next time I come in here, there had better be a female on this Galaxy Oversight Board. What eon are we living in, anyway?"

A hand shot up. "Um, Supreme Overseer?"

"Yes?"

"Um, Ralph, Madame Overseer. You're killing him. I'm quite sure that is a breach of your contract."

By the look on Ralph's face, she could tell that he wasn't sure at all. He was hoping though. He was hoping very thoroughly that he was right about the last part.

She smiled and then glared, daring them, any of them, to think anything as insulting as wobbly head now.

No? Didn't think so.

"You're right," she answered sweetly. "About not being allowed to kill any of the board members. It was written quite clearly into my contract."

His hand shot up again. She ignored it.

"However," she continued, "his heart is still beating, I assure you." She eased up a little on the pressure to allow his face to turn from a horrid purple to a slightly healthier reddish color. "I can feel it very clearly."

She released him. "He's fine. Somebody get him some water. And where's my coffee?"

A member of the wait staff burst into the room and hurried around the table, delivering the coffee.

"Thank you, dear," Soda said sweetly. Then she waited for the room to clear until it was just her and the board again.

"Does anybody else need me to check their pulse?"

She waited a beat. "No? Very well then. I only have one more question. Has anybody here actually read the Inquiry itself? The whole thing?"

A very worried mumbling spread across the room. From their blank expressions, Soda was certain the board had no idea what the Inquiry was about. No clue. *Idiots.* Her plan was completely safe. A flash of relief mixed with one of rage at having to be here at all.

"Let me get this straight," Soda said. Time to bring it home. "You call me here, under pretense of an Intergalactic Inquiry that you haven't even bothered to read. Then you question me about my contract? And demand that I be more transparent?"

She stood and rose to full height.

"Is that what you really want?" She was just gloating now. "For me to come to more of these useless meetings? Think long and hard before demanding my presence again."

Humiliating them might push them to read and understand the Inquiry itself, but she doubted it. They were lazy and stupid. And she'd made her point well enough.

She sat back down and sipped her coffee. It was perfect and perky and warm. And the timing was spot on too. This couldn't have gone better. Now she could get back to her plan. To her pretty pet, Drexyl. She had bigger things to deal with. She had to take care of Kirian. This whole Intergalactic Inquiry thing had to be nipped in the bud.

* * *

"DID you make it to the Overlord?" Brad asked Trisha. He leaned against the jail cell wall that separated the two of them. They had sat in silence for awhile in their adjacent cells.

"Nope," Trisha replied, holding her left wrist still. She had fallen on it in the takedown and now it was sore. Maybe even sprained. Could this day get any worse?

"First time being arrested?" he asked.

"Yep."

"You're doing pretty well, then. I hope it won't hurt your career," he said.

"No, it'll probably add to my cred. It may even help my thesis.

But not as much as a denial from the Overseer herself would have."

"So, who's going to bail us out?"

"Oh, my college has a satellite office here, they'll come and get us. I'll vouch for you."

"Thanks," he said. "You almost got there, you know. I heard the security people talking about it."

"Oh, I was close. It's true. I caught sight of her."

"You did?"

"Yup," Trisha said. "She was barely from me to that water cooler." She pointed. “She was right there in front of me. For a moment, I'm pretty sure we made eye contact.” She reflected on the encounter for a moment. “Oh, I'm sorry, but she looked an awful lot like an octopus to me."

"That's alright," he said.

“Thanks anyway, for trying to help me,” Trisha said. She pulled a business card out of her pocket with her good hand. "I'll be spending most of the next few days researching Celestial anyway, so if you hear anything, will you give me a call?"

* * *

SODA LAUGHED ALL the way back to her lair. She felt considerably better than she did on the trip to the board meeting. She had suspected that the board members were too stupid to figure out what was going on, and now they were too scared to as well. All she needed to do was get back to where she was happiest and comfortable, her lair. And also, to get out of the uncomfortable dress jeans.

She arrived and threw open the door. Drexyl was there, as always. She smiled at him.

"Good news. The board is a bunch of morons who couldn't understand the math. The Inquiry was utter Greek to them. And

I'm pretty sure that I scared them out of even trying to hire a translator. I think we're in the clear."

Drexyl deflated a little at the news.

He's just tired and pretty. He can't understand all of the nuances of being Supreme Overseer the way I can.

"And that brings us to our next very important topic. Reptar."

"Did I say Reptar?" Drexyl asked, "what I really meant was Ysmeoa. That's where the Intergalactic Inquiry originated from."

Damn him and the stars, he was obviously covering for Kirian. He had the Supreme Overseer, right here in front of him. Soda was trying to be patient and give him time to get over his crush, but she was starting to get irritated.

With a wave of a tentacle, she knocked him over and crossed to the console. "Well, let's just double check that information, shall we?"

She tapped the keypad and scanned through the details. "No," she said, pulling the now upright Drexyl toward her, "you were right the first time. It was Reptar. And who is it that we had recently on the planet of Reptar? Oh yeah. I believe that would be Kirian, Destroyer of Planets."

She waved her tentacles around dramatically when repeating Kirian's ridiculous nickname. "Oh yes, I know all about her self-made dark net mythology."

"What are you going to do?" He asked.

"You know, I threw a tentacle around the throat of a board member who was giving me trouble."

His eyes grew wide. "Is that legal? Did you kill him?"

"Well, there it is. That's why you are the smartest assistant I've ever had. Get right down to the heart of the matter, don't you? Anything up to actual death is, in fact, legal."

She laughed. "They really should have gotten a lawyer to look at my contract before signing it. But they were so happy to have a level 678 efficiency being passing through this galaxy, one thing led to another, and they just didn't care about the details. I said I might be persuaded to take the job, and before long they would have signed anything I put in front of them."

Happy memories.

"Anyway, so this guy that I'm strangling is turning all sorts of red and purple, right? And I watched the panic on the faces of the other board members. They're politically so powerful in this world and yet they're also so fragile. Watching helplessly as their colleague suffered."

"What happened next?"

"Well, they whined to me. 'It says in your contract you can't kill us'," she pantomimed their words. "And I smiled. Because," she slipped a tentacle between his legs, "my tentacles are so sensitive and they collect so very much data about everything that they touch, well I could feel his heart beating, all the way back through my own body. Every single beat. It started out strong and steady, but by the end it was thready and weak. Several board members vomited at the sight of it, but the heartbeat was there. I could hear it and I could feel it. I knew that he wasn't, in fact, dead."

She paused for a moment. His face had turned a ghastly white. "Drexyl, are you okay?"

"Fine," he lied, swallowing. "Go on."

"But let me tell you. The looks on their faces, they weren't at all sure he was going to make it. It really is a pity, you know, to let a cowardly weasel like that board member live and kill a useful agent like Kirian."

"But you can't kill her! You don't even know if she's the one who filed the Intergalactic Inquiry!"

Soda waved a tentacle around. "Oh, come on. There's no way it wasn't her. That would be an insane coincidence. Who else on Reptar was even capable of that sort of thing?"

"But why would she file that form? And why now? It doesn't make sense."

Soda thought about it. True, Kirian was brave but she wasn't that bright.

"Fine," she said, "I'll investigate it, but just to be sure, I'm destroying Reptar. This whole Inquiry thing has to be stopped in its tracks."

Chapter 17

The console chimed. It was a sound Ari had heard before. It was Kirian's boss. Remembering the Inquiry, a wave of fear hit her. She grabbed Kracken, who happened to be standing nearby and pulled him under the console with her out of sight. Fleek, on the other end of the room, heard it too. He grabbed Carpe and ducked around the corner. Five seconds later, when the familiar handsome face appeared on the screen, Kirian was at her usual chair, feet up on the console.

"Hi Drexyl," she said.

"Kirian! You're okay," he exhaled.

"No thanks to you people. The order said the planet wasn't going to be destroyed. What changed your minds?"

"Why would you hang around after the mission was completed?" Drexyl shot back.

A tentacle floated across the screen and wrapped itself around Drexyl's face, muffling whatever he was going to say next.

Ari stifled a gasp. As she peeked up at the screen from under the console, another figure slid front and center. It was the Octopus Overlord herself. She was a beautiful neon blue.

In the center of the tentacles was a misshapen head. The

head wobbled slightly back and forth continuously. Ari guessed that maybe the bulbous head was too heavy for the frame supporting it.

Ari found herself shaking her head back and forth in the exact opposite pattern in a subconscious attempt to cancel it out and keep it still. The movement made her queasy.

The octopus face eyed Kirian intensely. Kirian returned the gaze. Kirian had neither anger, surprise, nor defiance in her eyes, she was simply returning the creature's gaze without fear. Ari decided to ask Kirian what the trick was to that, because she had never got the knack.

"Enough. I ordered the attack on Reptar. I am, as you know, Tttssssorrarrddeehhhhaaaair, Supreme Overseer of the Galaxy. And I have some questions for you, Kirian Destroyer of Planets."

Ari inched herself up as high as she dared, to get a closer look at the mysterious and notoriously reclusive ruler of the Galaxy. Unless Ari was imagining things, the creature said the last part to Kirian sarcastically. Why try to kill your own employee, then call them up afterward and be snarky? Who does that?

"I guess that means you've been bored and poking around on the dark web." Kirian said, equally as mocking.

Ari wondered if the two of them had seen each other before. At the bar, it was coming back to her now, Kirian had mentioned wanting to kill her.

"Did you file an Intergalactic Inquiry on Reptar?" The octopus' gaze took on a new interest, and the bulbous head began to quiver rather than simply wobble.

"No," Kirian said.

Drexyl tried to yell something. Ari could almost make it out, but then the tentacle tightened further around his face and neck.

"But I know who did. I took care of it," Kirian continued. "I killed the being before it could cause more damage. You're welcome. Next time maybe you should ask before destroying the planet."

Ari watched as the Overlord, still quivering, considered Kirian's words. If Ari had to guess, this time the quivering would be rage. The whole idea of even trying to read that creature's hideous body language made her insides squirm, possibly even more than the space ship doing flips. She steadied herself, holding on to the leg of a console chair nearby.

The Overseer seemed to be mulling things over. "You just remember who works for whom here, Kirian," she said. Then she pressed a button with a tentacle on her console.

An electric buzzing erupted from Kirian's silver bracelet. Kirian's body tensed, and her teeth clenched. Then she screamed.

Ari fought back an urge to help. Kirian had covered for her having submitted the Intergalactic Inquiry, but if the Overseer saw her, she would know the truth.

The Overseer released the button. The buzzing stopped and Kirian slumped forward onto the console. Ari watched as the Overseer turned toward the purple-faced Drexyl and then the monitor went dead and switched back to a peaceful view of the stars.

Ari rushed forward to Kirian. Carpe and Fleek came around the corner.

Ari searched Kirian for a pulse. She found it and breathed a sigh of relief. "Do you believe she's a Celestial now?" Ari snapped at Carpe.

Fleek moved forward to help Ari check on Kirian.

"Let's get her into bed," said Ari, and the two of them gingerly carried her out of the main bridge area down the hall to her room.

Once that was done, Ari did the only thing she could think of under the circumstances.

"Ship meeting," she called when she and Fleek had rejoined everyone. The others were sitting in the bridge area of the ship eying each other suspiciously.

"You can't call a ship meeting," Fleek said, "you've barely been here longer than they have, and this is my ship. I get to call the meetings."

"You paid for this ship?"

"Yes."

"How?" Ari looked at the tall skinny figure with the shaggy blond Mohawk hair, blue lipstick, and ratty ironic t-shirt.

"None of your business," he said testily.

"Fine," Ari conceded, "if it's your ship, then you call the meeting."

"I will. We're having a meeting. Here on my ship."

Ari rolled her eyes.

"Why do we need a meeting?" Fleek whispered to her.

"Well, it appears we're stuck with these people for now." She eyed Carpe and Kracken. "Is this one of those customizable ships that can add extra space?"

"Oh," said Fleek. "Good point. I'm pretty sure I paid for that feature."

Ari knew that the ship right now had three bedrooms, one each for Kirian, Fleek, and Ari. She knew from the internet that higher end space ships often came with on-the-fly customizable floor plans, square footage not being a particularly big issue in space.

Fleek sat at the console, found the right settings, and tapped out some modifications. It didn't take very long. "There," he said, "two more rooms."

"Unless you'd like to bunk with me," Carpe said to Ari, adding a wink.

"I'm good for now, thanks."

A tsunami of physical and emotional exhaustion washed over Ari, the kind of overwhelming tiredness that came from knowing you should have died twice in the previous few days. There was also the whole thing where she submitted an Intergalactic Inquiry that apparently made her an enemy of the most powerful creature in the Galaxy. Even if the Octopus Overlord hadn't figured it out yet, it was just a matter of time.

All she wanted to do was collapse in her bed. That, and she wanted the door lock to work properly. She wasn't happy about her new ship mates, but this was her reality now and she was going to have to live with it.

Luckily, she no longer cared about anything but sleep. If anybody was planning on killing her while she slept, hopefully they would at least have the decency to be quiet about it.

So thinking, she made her way to her new and hopefully temporary room, locked the door, and collapsed into bed.

Chapter 18

When Ari finally awoke it was morning and quiet. The bedside clock told her she'd been asleep for at least ten hours. She wondered if anybody else on the ship was awake. Her head hurt, and her muscles were sore. She sat up and tried to think, but decided against it. Thinking was a bad idea.

A good idea was to get up and rummage through the galley and find some coffee.

She quietly unlocked her door and peeked outside into the rest of the ship. Nothing. Still in last night's clothes, she padded out to the galley.

There weren't very many non-bedroom doors on the craft, so the galley, which was next to the bridge, was easy to find. When she found it, she also found Fleek. He was poking around making coffee.

"Good morning," she said, hoping the coffee would taste similar to the delicious brew she'd had on Reptar. On the counter, there was a package of blue powder. She picked it up and inspected it.

"That's mine," said Fleek, and put the baggie into his robe

pocket. He poured them both a large glass mug of coffee and sat at the small kitchen nook in the corner.

Ari took the seat next across from him. "Sorry I didn't believe you about owning the ship yesterday," she said, "it's just that you look more like a..." Ari realized that there was no good way to end the sentence. She trailed off and hoped he wouldn't' notice.

"Like an underground musician?" he offered.

"What?"

"Is that what you thought I was?" He beamed at her, exhibiting a level of excitement Ari didn't believe herself capable of this early in the day. "Because that's what I am."

"Yes," said Ari, grabbing at the opportunity. "That's exactly it. I thought to myself, this guy is obviously an underground musician. But really, there's no money in being an underground musician. So, I was wondering where the money came from. For this ship."

Ari realized she was being nosy, but it seemed important to know what was going on in the place she was currently living. "I mean, if you don't mind me asking."

"You really want to know?"

"Yes," Ari said. "I do."

"Careful with that, you might want to slow down," Fleek said, nodding at her coffee. "You don't want to get addicted."

Ari pointed at the robe pocket he had placed the blue powder into. "You have your addictions, and I have mine."

He shrugged. "Fair enough. The Blue Pixie I have. It's first rate. You should try some. It would probably do you some good."

Ari scowled. "No thanks. I'm good as I am."

They sipped in silence for a while, Ari looking out at the dark, starry, night sky. It was the most peaceful she felt since, well since before the first planet blew up.

Was this what living in space was like? Peace followed by chaos and terror followed by peace again?

"So really," Ari said, in case he thought he had distracted her into forgetting. "How did you buy the ship?"

"I like you." Fleek decided it more than said it. "So, I'll tell you my secret. I'm a very famous hacker. Well, former hacker."

Ari studied his face, trying to figure out whether he was messing with her or not.

He held up a hand. "I know what you're thinking," he said. "I don't look or act like the type. That's true. But it was something I was always good at. Something I understood. Not the math of it, mind you, but the art of it. The concepts behind the math, you might say. It was like I could sense what people were trying to hide, like the secrets wanted me to find them."

Ari wondered how much of the Blue Pixie he had ingested and tried very hard not to roll her eyes. Why would he lie, though? It was the most preposterous thing she had ever heard. There was also an earnest persuasiveness about him that she liked.

"Does Kirian know your secret?"

"Of course she knows. That's how I bought this ship."

"It's a very nice ship, by the way," Ari said. "Thank you for letting me stay."

"You're welcome."

"So, you modified the whole ship, right on the fly, by adding those rooms for everybody. That's really cool."

"Oh, it's the newest technology," he said, "In fact, if it didn't have the most advanced pre-warp system in the galaxy we'd have never gotten out of range of the last planet's deletion. That was wild."

Ari rubbed a sore shoulder. "Yes, it certainly was. I gotta start holding on to things better next time that happens. Wait, you're a hacker, right?"

"Was. I'm a musician now. Covered that already." He took another sip and raised an eyebrow at her. His long blond

Mohawk flopped from one shoulder to the other with a gesture of his head that Ari guessed he practiced regularly in the mirror.

"Look, there's some information I really need. Do you think you can hack into Kirian's black spy watch?"

"What kind of information are we talking about? And why are you spying on Kirian?"

"Not on," said Ari, smiling, "for. I'd like all of the documents requested and submitted from her previous missions. And any and all info on how that stupid handcuff bracelet thing works. I'm going to try to free her."

Fleek's face froze for a moment. "You submitted the Intergalactic Inquiry, didn't you? Only somebody with that capability would even think of trying to free Kirian."

"Aye, that she did." Kracken had entered the galley and was pouring himself a mug. The booth was pretty small so he stood instead of trying to cram himself into a seat. "Thanks for having me aboard, Captain Fleek."

"Don't call me Captain," Fleek snapped. "It's just Fleek. And who's he again?" He looked to Ari, who shrugged.

"Some conspiracy theory resistance guy. Just met him yesterday. Kirian knows him, though. She can tell us more when she's awake."

"Hey," said Kracken, "we shared a dance."

"What about your guest?" Ari asked Fleek.

"Oh yeah, Carpe. He's a member of my band, now. I'm recruiting."

"I play the drums," Kracken volunteered.

"Not you," Fleek said.

"Whatever you say. Captain."

Carpe backed his way into the room with his hands up, followed by Kirian brandishing a short metal sword.

"Fleek, jog my memory. Who's this?" Kirian asked.

"That's Carpe, remember? He's my new bass player."

"Why was he lurking around my room?"

"Probably because he's never seen a Celestial before."

Kirian gave Carpe a dirty look, but she holstered the sword to her pajama bottom. Ari made a mental note to ask her about that later.

"This ship's getting crowded." Kirian passed Carpe without a further word, poured herself a mug, and finished off the pot.

Before anyone could speak, the nefarious brain-washing ring tone began to play in the adjacent bridge.

Kirian's face tensed. She put her mug down and turned to answer it. Ari remembered where she hid the little mirror in the drawer underneath after agreeing to Medusa the next session. She tried to dart into the bridge behind Kirian, but Fleek stood in her way shaking his head no, his face a mask of concern.

"It's too risky," he said, "you don't know what you're getting yourself into."

He was sweet and all, but he seriously underestimated how far Ari was willing to go once she had a plan. She ducked underneath him.

Free and clear, Ari dove underneath the console just as Kirian answered.

"Greetings, Kirian, are you alone?" the voice asked.

Ari, underneath, fumbled quietly in the drawer until she found the mirror.

"Why are you doing this to me?" Kirian asked.

"Whatever are you talking about?" the voice asked, smoothly.

Ari sucked in a breath for courage and snuck the mirror just over the edge of the console to get a peek at the screen. Kirian describing her nightmares came to mind and the possibility of seeing a giant Praying Mantis made her pause and suck in a breath.

She had read an article about it once. The species in question was called Andromeda Mantix, and its nickname was the "Preying Mantis." Cruel, deadly, and lazy, they were banished to a handful of planets on the fringes of the known universe.

Still, a plan was a plan, and curiosity eventually got the better of her.

"I'm talking about the stealing and the violence. And the blacking out. I know it's you that's causing it."

"You're a Celestial," the voice answered calmly. "It's what you do. How do you know that anything I'm doing is altering the natural course of your life?"

Ari adjusted the mirror slowly and carefully to avoid attention. The figure on the screen was indeed scanning the edges around Kirian for anyone else. Interesting. The figure looked normal. Humanoid. Small, thin and balding. Ari couldn't help but be disappointed. At least he wasn't a terrifying Preying Mantis.

"I'm afraid those are issues for your actual therapist, not me. I'm in charge of your Celestial affairs. And speaking of that, I'd like you to breathe out and look deeply into my eyes."

Ari could see that suddenly the figure's eyes flashed a feral green and then returned to normal. Kirian let out a breath as she was told and Ari saw her body tense and then relax. Ari swallowed and held her breath.

"Good, good," the voice said.

"Now, I need you to listen to me very closely. I have a lot of Celestials to get to and not much time. We have the constellation star activation symbol for theft and the dragon's head for violence. Those experiments have gone as planned. Today we are adding a new image. It's this Mantis head. Do you see it? If you see this symbol, you will revert immediately back to the level three consciousness that we've been working toward."

The mousy man got, in Ari's estimation, needlessly technical after that and the session went on for some time before he told Kirian's conscious mind to forget everything that he said as well as what he looked like when he snapped his fingers. He snapped his fingers and then disappeared.

Kirian came to and glanced at Ari who was still under the console.

"Well?"

"Good news," said Ari, "he's not a Preying Mantis. Yay. The bad news is that Fleek's totally right about him, you should absolutely find a new therapist."

Chapter 19

Floyd lay slumped on the luxurious sofa in his exclusive high-rise condo trying to figure out what to do about the Celestial army slipping from his grasp. He stood and crossed to the giant window with a view overlooking the city and tried to come up with ideas.

Earlier, he had stalked and killed something, which made him feel better. It also made him hungry. He decided to call out for pizza. Then he sat back on his couch and flipped through television channels waiting for it to arrive.

He stopped flipping channels. Then he used the remote to go back; sure he had seen something familiar several channels ago. He couldn't believe it. There, on the television screen, was Soda.

He turned up the volume. As he did so, his doorbell rang. *Finally.* He jumped up and ran to the door. The delivery kid stood with his two extra-large supreme pizzas.

"Took you thirty-five minutes, so it's free," Floyd said.

The kid looked down at his watch. "It's only been seventeen minutes, mister."

Floyd looked around the hallway to make sure nobody else was around. Then he opened his eyes, pulling them wider and larger than beings in this galaxy were allowed, then he changed the hue to incandescent lime green.

"Hey, mister," the pizza guy said, staring, "are you okay?"

The pizza kid had seen the green flash of his eyes and was ensnared now and swaying slightly from side to side.

"You meant to say that the pizza was late and it's free," Floyd said again.

"The pizza was late," pizza boy repeated, "and it's free."

"Great," said Floyd. He took the pizza and slammed the door. He took several steps toward the television.

"Hey, what about my tip?" the pizza boy's voice asked through the door.

"You've got ten seconds to get out of here, scofflaw before I call security and have you thrown out of the building!" Floyd yelled angrily; then he turned up the television volume again to drown out any follow up questions.

A square-headed news anchor sat next to a stock image of the Neon Octopus Overlord. *That's not what she looks like,* he thought. Her head is more bulbous. And you certainly don't know her like I do.

“A historic Intergalactic Governing Board Meeting was held today," the news anchor said, "with the notoriously reclusive Octopus Overseer of the Galaxy because of an Intergalactic Inquiry that was filed last week. Despite the unprecedented interest, no press was allowed into the meeting. Additionally, the Overseer didn't answer any questions."

The news station then ran a video clip of a young woman who appeared to be holding a microphone running toward the Octopus Overlord only to be taken down hard by half a dozen security guards.

"Oof. That had to hurt," Floyd said to himself between bites of pizza.

The newscaster, now back on screen, continued. "A limited transcript of the meeting, approved by the Overseer, will be released to the public tomorrow."

Floyd had seen enough. He switched off the television. "Such a cushy gig," he said, jealous, "especially when you get to make up all the rules. And how dare she treat me this way."

Something he thought earlier came back. They don't know her like I do. This Intergalactic Inquiry has created quite a stir. It was probably very distracting. And he knew where the next Celestial mission was going to be.

What if he snuck over there and broke the communications disrupter she used to conceal the Celestial missions? Then the whole Galaxy would know what she was up to.

She thinks she's busy now?

Then she'd have endless questions to answer and possible criminal charges. With all of that going on she probably wouldn't have time to destroy her Celestial army. He gobbled down his pizza and set his plan in motion.

Chapter 20

Soda woke from her extra deep sleep refreshed and energized. She looked in the mirror. As expected, she was at least four inches taller. How clever she had been to use a form altering disguise capable of adapting to new threat levels.

No, Soda, you have nothing to worry about. And soon those stupid Staars will have no idea where you are.

She turned her gaze to Drexyl, sleeping in the corner. He was as peaceful and beautiful as ever. "Sleep, my love," she whispered, waving a tentacle over his sleeping form. He'd now sleep through anything that happened. And what was about to happen would upset him if he saw or heard it.

These people had no idea what power she possessed. She'd been hibernating in low power mode this entire time. It had taken zero effort to keep this galaxy going.

She slithered over to the console, happy to be more herself. About time she had a challenge. She tapped in the contact info for Kirian, Destroyer of Planets.

Don't make me laugh.

Kirian had never once destroyed a planet. It was blatant false advertising.

The whole Celestial myth was a thing of beauty. It was easily her best idea. Where do you hide a nefarious, top-secret, planet-deleting program from a slightly civilized galaxy? In plain sight, of course. She leaked the information to a few crack pots. Let them make fools of themselves. Then she unleashed a wave of editorials making merciless fun of the crackpots, assuring they would never again be taken seriously. It was all too easy.

Kirian appeared on the monitor. "Yes, your Supreme Overlord? Hey, where's the other guy?"

"Hello, Kirian. We need to talk."

"I don't believe I ever fully caught your name. Could you repeat it, please?"

Soda thought about this. She had adopted Soda as her name in this galaxy because of Drexyl, but so far, the name existed only in her head and on his lips. Mmmmm. She toyed with the idea of using it with Kirian. One, because Kirian would soon be dead, so it didn't matter. Two, because she wanted to hear what it sounded like out loud coming from someone other than Drexyl. And three, because nobody in this galaxy could pronounce the real thing anyway.

"You may call me Soda," the Octopus Overseer said. "Well?"

"Well, what?" Kirian looked confused.

"Call me Soda."

"Um," said Kirian. "Hello, Soda."

Soda processed for a moment.

Yes, that will do just fine. It rolls right off of the tongue, it's easy for these idiots to pronounce, and it also has sentimental value. Soda it is.

Soda fixed Kirian with a harsh stare. "I don't like you. Drexyl does. Drexyl believes that you're not involved in this whole Intergalactic Inquiry thing. What matters, though, is that I need you out of my way. So here's what's going to happen."

She buzzed Kirian's handcuff, causing a jolt of electricity, and watched the effect. Kirian jumped and sizzled and gritted her teeth. Most exciting. She halted the electricity. Then she looked around. "Hey, is Ari around? This concerns her too."

"I have no idea who you're talking about," Kirian answered.

"Oh, we're way past that," Soda cooed. "You're going to your next mission, as planned," Soda continued, "and then both you and the planet are going down. Permanently. That is unless the smarty-pants whose life you saved decides to try and return the favor and help you. But I guess she's already fled. Am I right?"

"I'm right here," Ari said, entering the screen.

"Good. I filed a galaxy-wide most wanted bulletin with a huge price on your head. So even if you run, you won't be able to hide."

Soda scanned Kirian's face for fear or panic. There wasn't any. Good. At least Kirian wasn't going to take all the fun out of it. "I mean, I did officially plan to terminate you with the rest of the Celestials after the next mission anyway, but I figured why wait? Spoiler alert, this will be your last mission."

"Which planet?" Kirian asked.

"Regulus."

Soda looked at her console clock. "I'd get to work if I were you. You only have a few hours to get there. Happy final mission, Kirian, Destroyer of Planets."

"What did you do with Drexyl?" Kirian asked.

"Oh, don't worry, he's fine."

Soda smiled and ended the transmission.

Then she glanced over at Drexyl's sleeping form. He had, by design, missed the whole thing. She released him from his spell, and he continued sleeping peacefully anyway. She nestled back into bed. There would be plenty of time later to wake him for the big Kirian finale.

* * *

THE CONSOLE WENT DARK. Ari moved first, checking on Kirian, who looked a little dazed after the latest electric shock.

Ari felt bad. It was her fault, after all. She'd honestly had no idea what kind of mess the Intergalactic Inquiry would cause, or what forces it would set into motion. And now she was a wanted fugitive.

"Kirian. Let me see those bracelets."

Kirian held them out for her; her hands were still trembling.

“Ouch,” Kirian said, “does anybody on this ship have any alcohol?”

"Fleek, can you get us to that planet?"

"Autopilot. I've got stuff to do," he said it while disappearing around the corner with Carpe. Kracken was still lurking in the galley doorway.

"We've got a lot of work to do here, for Kirian," Ari said angrily. "Why aren't you people helping?"

Kirian stared at her. "They're afraid. And they should be. The question is, why are you still here? Why don't you sensibly and logically run away? Soda was right. You should go, no sense in all of us dying. I'm already halfway there with the electric shock and the brainwashing anyway."

Ari looked her in the eye. "Because I can do it. I can figure this out."

"Ari," Kirian said. "You should go live your life. That Octopus took me away from my home world. She killed me a long time ago. It's only now catching up, you see."

"I'm telling you, I can do this," Ari said, turning one of Kirian's bracelets over in her hand. What she wouldn't give for a decent spectrograph. "Some of this is my fault. And besides, she'll eventually get me too if I can't stop her. If we split up, she'll just kill us separately. Hey, do you have any spectrographs around?"

“Top left drawer," Kirian said nodding at a cabinet next to the navigation console. "And you can leave Fleek alone; I can set an autopilot." Kirian tapped some coordinates into the console. "I just can't free-fly the thing."

Kracken joined them. "The best way to foil her, lass, is to file another report. Hit her where it hurts."

"No," Ari said. "There's no time. I have to figure out how to help Kirian."

"Look, that psycho octopus is going to kill Kirian. There's no reason the rest of us have to go with her. You could sneak off to a safe planet, finish your research, and then really have a go at her."

"Kracken's got a point," Kirian said.

"No way," Ari turned to Kracken. "I'm not giving up on this Inquiry issue either, but when I go at her with paperwork, it's got to be perfect. You know that. Or maybe you don't; I don't care. Hold this." She handed the spectrograph to Kracken while holding Kirian's bracelet at the different angles needed to get a proper readout. Kracken obliged until the little gizmo beeped. The console darkened again, and the results appeared.

Ari sat down next to Kirian to study the screen.

"What's all that mean?" Kirian asked.

"The bracelet's made out of a metal alloy. Obviously, it's good at conducting electricity. Probably nearly indestructible because it looks from its properties as though it's magnetically sealed."

"Makes sense. Nearly cut my arm off trying to get it off," Kirian said. "Look, I don't think it's possible, Ari. Not even you can figure this out in the time frame that we're talking about. You should be making other plans."

Carpe returned to the bridge of the ship. "What are you up to now?"

Ari looked at him. "Carpe, you're a bass player, right?"

"Yes. At the moment."

"And your former occupation was..."

"Organized Crime Enforcer, why?"

Ari smiled. "Did you guys ever use anything like this on people?" She pointed at one of Kirian's bracelets.

Carpe crossed to Kirian, knelt, and looked carefully at it. "Is this what they use to zap you full of electricity?"

"Yep. I mean, for being a prisoner it's not always the worst gig in the world. I get to travel, unlimited money, and all I have to do is everything they say, or I get electrocuted."

"Sign me up," Carpe said, still looking at the bracelet.

"I have no idea what that screen is saying," Carpe said, looking at the readout from the spectrograph, "but we did have something like this. I don't think it was your fancy alloy, just whatever metals were hanging around our location. Wasn't too much trouble either to pair them with sensors and link them to genetic code. Once that's done, no matter where the prisoner is, you press the button, and they get some juice. Very effective." He looked at Kirian. "Sorry."

Ari thought about this. "Presumably then, the electricity could go both ways?"

Carpe thought about it. "Never happened. Never even considered it. But I suppose you could be right."

"How'd you get them off?" Ari asked.

"Can't help you there," he answered. "We didn't."

Ari huffed in frustration at him, standing up. "It's illegal, everywhere in the galaxy, to make private prisoners."

"Aye," he answered, "it's illegal to destroy planets as well."

"He's got you there, Ari," Kirian said.

Fleek walked onto the bridge.

"I thought you had more important things to do," Ari said.

"I do. Recruiting. For the band. I had to step up my timeline due to recent events." He glared at Ari.

"Recruiting? For the band? You heartless bastard..."

Fleek held a hand out to her, stopping her in mid-sentence. He crossed the room and got in her face. "Look, new girl. You deal with problems your way, and I'll deal with them mine. But since you're so logical, let's follow this through to its conclusion. You guys go to the planet. You try to save it, and you try to save Kirian. Let's say you succeed. And you get back to my ship."

Ari had no idea what was going on. She nodded anyway.

"So, what does that octopus thing do next? She blows up my beautiful ship, right? I mean, what's to stop her? Everything she's ever done has been in secret. Everything. Including tonight's threat. This Overseer obviously values her privacy.

So, let's say you succeed."

He turned to Kirian again. "Fingers crossed. And you get back to the ship and this ship," he said, holding his hands out dramatically, "is now the most famous, the most rocking, the most live streamed ship in the galaxy. Then what do you think she does? Well, not blow it up is my guess. In conclusion, I'm doing my part. So let me work and stop interrupting me."

Ari blinked at him, opened her mouth and shut it again. "That's your plan?"

"Yes."

"Your plan," she began again, sure she had misheard, "is to form a band, and broadcast your song."

"Yes."

"And become instantly famous?"

"Right again."

"So, the Overseer will be impressed or shy or who knows, maybe she's a music lover. At any rate, she'll decide not to destroy us."

"I think it's kind of perfect, don't you?"

"That may be the most conceited, unrealistic plan I've ever heard. There's not a snowball's chance in a black hole of all of that happening, no matter how good your song is."

"Says you."

"Exactly," said Ari, crossing her arms, "says me. Why can't you do something useful? Like hacking into the Overseer's computer or helping me with the files I need?"

"Absolutely not."

"Of course not," said Ari.

Fleek grabbed Carpe and disappeared again.

Ari watched them go. "Kirian, why in stars are you enjoying this?"

Kirian seemed surprised by the question. "Up until recently, there was no Fleek. For years it was just me flying around the galaxy on a little ship drinking wine, watching television and ducking planetary explosions by myself. Like, I said, not the worst gig ever, but not great either. Then Fleek talked me into saving him. He really is persuasive. Then I saved you. Now I live on a ship full of people, some of whom aren't jumping off just yet even in the face of danger." She smiled. "At least I'm going to go out with friends."

Chapter 21

Ari re-read the spectrograph.

Alloy metal with an electromagnetic lock.

What was she supposed to do about that?

Kracken. He had to be of some use.

"You, crazy conspiracy theorist." She got in his face, or ten inches underneath it anyway. He got the point. "You get a hold of your associates. Find out everything you can about these stupid handcuffs."

Carpe came out of Fleek's room again and raised an eyebrow at Ari. "All I'm saying, is that you have crime boss written all over you."

"Doubt it," Ari said, although she was starting to wonder herself. "Carpe, you guys used these too. If you could get any useful information at all, I'd appreciate it. Specifications, alloy proportions, weaknesses, strengths, anything."

"Strengths?" Carpe asked. "Why would you be interested in the strength of something you're trying to break?"

"Strengths and weaknesses," Ari answered, running a hand through her hair. "They're often related."

Carpe looked surprised for a moment. Then he grabbed his

cell phone and disappeared. Ari glared at Kracken until he did the same. Then it was just Ari and Kirian, who still sat at the console. Ari heaved herself into the chair next to her.

Kirian smiled broadly. "I wish I could go back and change things."

"You can only change the present and the future," Ari mused, barely audible.

"You're just full of those, aren't you?"

"Look, Kirian. I don't care what you've done. You saved me. I'm more interested in your future than your past. That's all. It's the way I have to look at things. Especially on a deadline."

"Look at you. Out in space. Ordering ex-organized crime lackeys around..."

"Just trying to help."

"I'll admit it was just a hunch at first. I had no idea how smart you really were," Kirian continued. "It only took a few days for you to jolt the Overseer into a murderous rage. I love it. And it looks like you're not done yet."

"Stars," Ari said, looking at the on-screen countdown timer. "We're almost there."

Kirian got up and headed to her room as Carpe entered on his way to the galley. Ari hoped to have a few minutes alone with her thoughts, but Carpe cleared his throat.

“One guy did get out of the handcuff.” He scooped up several bags of snacks and headed back to re-join Fleek.

Ari stood and crossed to him. “What was that? Did you say something about somebody getting free of the handcuff?”

"Yeah. That he got free of the handcuff."

"Specifically. Any details would be helpful."

"We assume he got free anyway. We found the cuff, but not the guy."

"Was the cuff broken?"

"No."

"Could he have wriggled his hand out?"

"I love that word, wriggled," Carpe mused.

Ari ignored him. The ship pitched suddenly. She leaned forward and grabbed hold of one of the console chairs. *Ha. I'm finally getting the hang of this.*

Then the ship lurched forward and did another front flip. Ari lost her grip on the chair, but didn't fall very far due to the ship's momentum. She was getting tired of her stomach having out of body experiences. The ship steadied itself.

"I don't think he wriggled out," Carpe continued. "The handcuffs have a magnetic seal. There was also no tissue and no blood."

Stars. That was going to be her next question.

"Hey," said Carpe, snapping his fingers, "we hired a specialist to come and inspect the handcuff, and he said the only thing he could think of was maybe it was a burst of high powered electromagnetic something." He made a gesture with his hand indicating the whole thing was over his head.

"Electromagnetic waves?" Ari suggested.

He nodded.

Interesting.

The ship lurched to a stop. Ari looked at the landscape through the console. There were forests and buildings and tall, angular bipeds walking around.

Ari turned to see Kirian re-enter the bridge. She was dressed differently. She had jeans, a grey t-shirt, and a black jacket- presumably to have a place to keep her weapons. Her long dark hair was pulled into a ponytail. She looked ready for battle.

* * *

ARI FRANTICALLY RESEARCHED everything she could find, both real and crackpot, about any type of metallic handcuff similar to the ones Kirian wore.

Fleek came up behind her, making her start. "You really are serious about helping her?"

"Yes."

"Well, you won't find the information you're looking for there," he said, a new mug of coffee steaming in his hand.

"Fine," she said. "Where can I find the information that I need?"

"The dark net, of course. You won't find out how to remove an explicitly illegal handcuff the Neon Octopus Overlord is using for nefarious reasons on the regular net. Duh."

The Dark Net. She should have considered that. As a bureaucrat, she was trained to use only verified sources of information.

It never even occurred to her to use an unofficial source, much less for something so important. She was really off-roading now. It was worth a try anyway, leave no stone unturned and all that.

"So how do I get onto the dark net?"

He smirked. "Never been on it? I figured as much. That's what I'm here for."

She let him set up her computer and ducked into the galley to get more coffee of her own.

As soon as Ari returned, full steaming mug in her hand, Kracken was standing between her and the computer Fleek had finished customizing. She leaned around Kracken to thank Fleek.

"Your computer milady." Fleek bowed.

"Hey, thank you, Fleek. How's recruiting going?"

"Great, thanks."

Kracken was shifting his weight from foot to foot, visibly annoyed at being ignored.

"I have to ask," Ari said, "Why on earth do you think that one song is going to make you famous? I mean, I guess on some level all musicians want to be famous, but only a small subset really believe it's going to happen, and fewer still have it actually come true. The odds are, well, that you're more likely to have a space fairy pop in and sprinkle dust on your head and make you famous than to hit it big in the music industry nowadays."

"If you know any space fairies, tell them I'm game." Fleek showed her that little boy smile trapped in the persona of the underground musician and disappeared.

Ari sighed, sat, and turned her attention to the dark net.

"It's all a waste of time," Kracken said, close enough to whisper in her ear, "you need to file a Complaint against the Overseer before it's too late. And here we are wasting time on metal handcuffs and musicians and..." He waved an arm, having run out of steam and lost his point.

"This again?" Ari asked. "Hey, no problem, you can get off the ship any time you want, and your conspiracy crackpot people can pick you up."

"You know that's not what I mean."

"It's what I mean. If you don't have any useful information for me, then at least get out of my way," Ari shot back.

He knelt beside her. She wished he would just go away, but she tried to concentrate despite him. She knew from experience that if she let him know he was bothering her, it would only make matters worse.

"Hey," he said, "what you're not doing here is thinking big picture. Anything can happen in the next few minutes."

Ari smiled. She took a long sip from her mug. "Yeah, that's what I'm counting on."

Kracken huffed and walked away. Finally. She resumed her research.

About that guy who got out of his handcuff..." a voice behind her made her start again. It wasn't Kracken though, this time, it was Carpe.

She wheeled viciously, a move that would have probably gotten her killed if he was in his past life. He raised an eyebrow at her.

"What?"

"Research not going as well as you had hoped?"

Ari hated to admit it, but he was right. Having never been on the Dark Net she expected it to be a useful and plentiful treasure trove of underground information. As it was, it was simply filled with porn, violence, and fractals.

"No, it isn't. I expected a lot more information. Frankly, there was more, if dubious information, on the regular web at disreputable sites."

"That sounds right." He heaved himself into a nearby chair.

Ari went to take a sip from her mug, but was it dry again. Stars. "Oh, what were you saying?" She was at a standstill anyway.

"Yeah, about the guy who possibly got out of the handcuff," he began again, rubbing his green chin with his hand. "We found the cuff, but not the man. I remembered some details. We did a system-wide search for the guy." He leaned into her. "Very serious. Called in our chips and got the regular cops to help out. If one guy gets away, well, then that's all any of them can think about. Then you've got problems. You see where I'm going with this?"

Ari thought about it. "You're saying if I find a way to free Kirian, it will cause problems, real problems, for the Overseer."

"Two birds with one stone."

"And why do you care, exactly?"

"Ah, good question. Knew it would come up eventually. Whose team am I on?"

"Well?"

"I'm on team Mayhem. The Overseer deserves what she gets, if you ask me. She's worse than we were when I was in organized crime. We were bottom feeders, to be sure, but there's room for bottom feeders in the ecosystem. We were naturally occurring, you see. Now her? She's something else. Not sure what, exactly, but it's bad business."

Ari thought about it. Kirian was a powerful prisoner. Kracken was a crackpot. Fleek was an oddball. But this guy had a grounded feel about him. As odd as it was, his was the closest thing to her reality. In some way, his old life must have made some sort of sense. But why abandon it to join Fleek? So far, she just couldn't see it.

Fleek returned, as if on cue, with a set of headphones. The kind she hated, the ones that wrapped around one's head and gave an immersive experience. She liked ear buds so she could have access to outside stimuli. He placed them on her head. She shook her head and tried to object, but he wouldn't have it.

"I have a ton of things to do," she said. It was true. It was also true that she had hit a dead end and wasn't getting anywhere anyway, she just didn't want to admit it.

"Relax," Fleek said. "It's just one song. What's the worst that could happen?"

He asked it with a particularly mischievous glint in his eye and pressed play.

Ari turned angrily toward the console which was currently showing the planet Regulus, and away from the eyes of both Fleek and Kracken. The music thumped to life in her ears, and the immersion took over.

* * *

"KIRIAN, how long before we know when everything on Regulus is going to start?" Ari asked.

"If the past is any indication," Kirian answered, "we're going to know much sooner than later. Hey, Ari? It's not going to be pretty. You should stay on the ship."

"Aye," said Kracken. "You should."

"Nobody asked you," Ari said. "So, Fleek and Carpe are staying here, right?"

"Right."

"And what about you?" Ari turned to Kracken. "Staying or going?"

"Not sure yet," he answered.

"Figures."

Kirian handed her a small pen-sized object.

"What is it?"

"It's a Stingr. It's a sword that works with light and heat. Very effective, very lethal. I have several, and I use them against the TPHWs because the waves of creatures that it creates can't feel fear. On living beings, though," she said, bringing out a shorter, curved metal sword, "nothing intimidates like sharp steel."

"Aye," Carpe said. "That's true enough."

Ari got an idea. The TPHWs. The waves of creatures. The energy needed. Electromagnetic energy. Maybe she could make it all work. She sat down at the computer.

The whole ship rattled, and there was a loud noise on Regulus.

Fleek came out from his room without a word and adjusted the view on the console manually. Together they searched for the source of the explosion. What they were looking for wasn't hard to spot.

A plume of smoke snaked to the sky from the center of what looked like a crowded downtown. The wave of surprise and panic in the population was just beginning.

"That's my cue," said Kirian. "Hey, this time, ironically, I get to try to save a planet."

Ari stopped looking at the console and frantically went back to work. "Be careful, Kirian. I'll catch up. I just got some new ideas. I'll be right behind you. And good luck."

Kirian tapped coordinates into the system, judging the approximate location of the explosion for the portal. Then she walked out through it and into the unknown.

The only thing Ari could do for her now was focus. Research. What she did best. *I got this.*

First, she completed chemical, elemental, and electromagnetic scans of the city under attack. When they were done, she broke into a broad smile. The scans had given her an idea. *Oh, I'm on to you Overseer.*

She needed another spectrograph. As she crossed the room to retrieve it, Kracken stood directly in front of her. She shot him an annoyed look, but instead of backing up in surprise and apology, he held his ground, staring down at her.

"Oh, there you are. Found you," Ari said sarcastically, trying to go around him. "I think I found something. I might even have a plan, but we're going to have to act fast, there's not much time to gather what we need. Are you coming with me? You don't have a mini torch, do you? That would come in really handy right about now..."

"Can't let you do that," Kracken said.

"I know you don't want me to leave and help Kirian, but that's too bad. Besides, this has the potential to hurt the Neon Octopus..." Ari had a lot more in her arsenal ready to argue with him, but that's when she saw the gun in his hand.

It was pointed at her head. *Not again.* "What are you doing?" Ari raised her hands. "I said I found a way to help."

He blinked at her, but didn't say anything.

Ari ran through the entirety of the past few days in her mind like a movie, slowing down when it got to the parts with Kracken. She thought the whole thing through and then shook her head.

"You didn't show up until after I filed the Intergalactic Inquiry." He let her continue. "You've been shadowing Kirian, but you're not part of the conspiracy group, are you?"

She hit her forehead with her hand, then held it in the air again. "No, you've been too quiet for that. Real conspiracy theorists believe in their cause. They won't shut up. That means you're working for the Overseer." She glanced at his wrists. "No handcuffs."

She looked up at him in surprise. "You're doing it on purpose?"

"You're coming with me, now, love," he said, motioning with the gun.

Ari didn't move. She wasn't done.

"Wait. You tried to kidnap me on Reptar. You couldn't blow your cover, and it paid off big time. You know about me. You know about all of us."

Ari started to hyperventilate. Her gaze went to the screen showing the planet where another commotion had begun. Kirian had two light Stingrs out against an oncoming horde of TPHWs.

"And Kirian? What about her?"

"Trust me, love. Kirian doesn't have a chance. She's dead already. But you don't have to be. Just come with me."

Ari heard a scream from Kirian on the console behind her and turned again to see what was happening.

Something hard hit her in the back of the head. Her knees went wobbly.

Kracken.

She had seen characters get hit in the head with a gun a million times on television, but had never experienced it in real life. She wasn't a fan.

First, there was the shock that someone had done it to you, then the explosion of pain in your head, and then everything began to fade. She turned toward her attacker, but Kracken wasn't looking at her anymore, he was turned to the side where a familiar face with two sets of arms hit him in the chest.

The two started to wrestle. A yell echoed and then faded, along with everything else. The words "get him, Carpe" floated around her consciousness with angry thoughts about guns and metal and people she thought were friends.

Chapter 22

Drexyl woke with a start. He didn't know why, but the hair on his arms were standing on end. He looked around and listened. Nothing. At least nothing out of the ordinary. It was more of a feeling. Having nothing else to focus on, he glanced at Soda sleeping in the corner. He did a double take, then blinked. Either Soda had changed and gotten bigger overnight, or another being had taken her place.

He must have shuffled his feet too loudly, because a wobbly eye popped open.

"Drexyl. Good morning." She inched her bulbous head higher, then stretched her tentacles.

"Soda?"

"Oh yes," Soda said, looking over herself. "You noticed. I've begun to change."

"What do you mean change? What's happening?"

"Oh, don't be alarmed, darling. Comes with the territory when one awakens from millennia in hibernation. Oh, how confused you look right now. There are a lot more surprises coming, I assure you. The first is your beloved Kirian. Switch on the monitor; she's about to have a very bad day."

Drexyl rubbed the sleep out of his eyes. "What's going on with Kirian? What did I miss?"

Soda's mouth stretched into a horrible smile. Maybe it was because her face was bigger, maybe it was because the longer lips curled into a more feral position, or maybe it was just because of the dark-colored hairs jutting from her face. He recoiled in horror as the tentacles came for him. That hadn't changed. Staars or no staars, the tentacles always came for him.

* * *

FLEEK LEFT Ari and returned to his room where his new lead guitarist, Marco materialized.

"Hello, Marco."

Drummer. It's the only thing the band still needed. It's true, he could go the synthetic route, but it went against the very spirit of the thing. Oh yeah. The studio. They couldn't broadcast without a studio. He headed back to his computer. He tapped in the code for the studio. A large room bowed off the end of the ship beyond his bedroom.

"Marco, the bass player's busy right now. We're out of time, and we need a drummer."

"I know a guy," Marco said. "But I don't think he'd do it. No way he'll broadcast live. His boss will see him and kill him. In fact, all of us are taking a really big chance here."

"The good news is that I've got us covered." Fleek led him back toward the new broadcast studio.

Marco chased after him. "What do you mean you have us covered? From death?"

"No, sorry mate. I'm good, but I'm not that good. I hacked us a bunch of new, hard core, rocker avatars."

"What?"

"Check it out," Fleek said. He brought up his computer, placed a sticker on Marco, and pushed him up onto the stage. "Go ahead and play."

As soon as Marco stepped onto the stage, he stopped being a Tillip—a squattish gray creature with spikes on his head—and morphed into a slimy, tall, long haired purple Kaleo.

"No way," he said, totally impressed.

"So, do you think your friend will be our drummer if I can protect his identity?"

Marco nodded. "Yes, absolutely, man."

"Great. Have him here in five minutes."

This music, this song was going to be a positive force in the galaxy, he just knew it. He didn't know how it could help Kirian; he just knew that it couldn't possibly hurt. And the fractals had never led him wrong. And the Oracle believed in him. Fleek couldn't say it out loud, but he simply believed.

* * *

TRISHA WAS NOW twenty hours into her research. It was horrible and involved dark net searches and conspiracy websites. The images would probably stay with her forever.

Thanks a lot, thesis.

She stopped for a minute and rubbed her face with her hands. A text notification buzzed. She glanced at the time: 3:47 in the morning? Who in stars name could that be?

It was a text from Brad.

Something's going down soon on Regulus. You said you wanted to know. Are you in or out?

She thought about it for a moment. If she stayed awake for the next—she rechecked her watch—forty hours she might have a chance of turning in her thesis on time.

Why did she do this to herself? Then she had an idea. There were shortcuts for this assignment, it was why she tried to interview the Octopus Overseer.

If she had been able to get one in-person quote from an official that important, her the thesis would have been complete. There was a points system to these things. In fact, just visiting the Capital in Arcturis City had earned her more points than the last week combined. It hit her in her sleep deprived state that the whole process was a video game and she was trying to get the high score.

She looked up the points system again. Leaving the planet to do the in-person research would get her, oh, three thousand or so points, along with the twenty-five hundred she received for going to the Capital. That combined with the work she had done in the previous twenty hours or so would put her—hang on, math hurting brain at this point—ten points over the minimum!

She re-ran the calculations, not trusting the math in her sleep-deprived state. It checked out. All she had to do was document this conspiracy theorist tipping her off, show up on Regulus, poke around a little, and she'd be done.

Of course, her bank accounts were dwindling fast, and her credit cards were maxed out, but portal service to Regulus wasn't too expensive, and once she'd finished her thesis she could graduate and start making money instead of just spending it.

There was a radical concept.

She texted Brad back, hoping soon meant soon or she might just sleep through anything that happened.

Ok, I'm in. See you in a couple of hours. Where do you want to meet?

Another text arrived: *When it Pours coffee house on Main St.*

* * *

KIRIAN STRODE into the middle of the city and smiled. The sun warmed her face, and a gentle breeze rustled her hair. The planet had a striking natural beauty. It was a good place to die.

She hadn't yet heard the humming of the TPHWs, so she took

her time. Duster off, skin glistening in the sun. She stuffed Stingrs into her jeans pockets and decided to start the battle with her curved scimitar. She kissed the flat end at the tip of the blade and lifted it toward the sun, in tribute, the way they used to do on her planet before it was destroyed. She took a deep breath. *Bring it.*

Then she heard the familiar hum of the weapons. Only this time it sounded different. Louder and clearer. At least twice the normal number of creatures appeared before her. Kirian squinted at her opponents and tightened her grip on the handle.

Something flew past her. She wheeled around to face it with her scimitar. It wasn't an opponent; it was a drone camera.

What's going on?

She scanned the skies and found that drone cameras were flying all over. Was the overseer filming the whole thing?

Kirian didn't have time to finish that thought. The creatures in front of her charged.

Chapter 23

Floyd grumbled as he made his way to the Arcturis City transit with all the other commuters. He liked his high rise and his luxury and hated mixing with the masses. Happily, he wasn't taking the actual portals; he had his own private ship waiting. If things went south on Regulus, he was prepared.

All his research had pointed to one conclusion. That it wouldn't be difficult to blow a hole in Soda's communications disrupter field, but it would have to be done from the inside, from the planet's surface.

In other words, work. It wasn't his style. But it would make a lot more work for Soda, so he smiled and continued worming his way forward in line.

Floyd smiled at the irony. He wanted the Celestial army to take care of his dirty work in much the same way Soda was using them to do hers. However, at this point, hypnotherapy wouldn't work for complex tasks, and the Celestials weren't yet his army to command.

He arrived at dock 42B and nodded to the Captain as he boarded.

"Immediate travel to Regulus in sector 872, sir. Is that correct?"

"Correct," Floyd answered. He took his seat and buckled up.

"Shouldn't take too long," the Captain said.

Floyd took out his phone and played the black-hole filling matching game that everybody was talking about. It passed the time just fine.

A little while later, the Captain announced they were hovering in orbit half a Urillian Click from Regulus, the far end of the limit of Floyd's portable, extra-long-range portal. This was the tricky part; he needed to convince the pilot to stay put no matter what he heard or saw.

If he were successful in breaking Soda's communications blocker, all hell would break loose. Then the Captain would know he was in danger and he'd probably want to warp out of the area pronto. If Floyd were unsuccessful, the Captain would be blissfully unaware and yet in lots more danger of blowing up.

He stood and faced the Captain, forcing himself to smile. "What I need you to do is stay right here for a while until I return."

"Got it," said the Captain.

"Because it's a fixed location, long distance portal."

"Uh-huh."

"And because if I try to return and you've gone off somewhere, I'll be jumping into open space."

"Exactly."

"And I'll die," Floyd said, underlining the point and adding a great big exclamation mark.

The Captain wasn't particularly engaged with the actual situation Floyd was trying very hard to impress upon him. In fact, he was replying to Floyd while texting on his phone.

Floyd decided his current approach wasn't working. He opened his eyes bigger and engaged them in hypnotherapy.

The Captain, already addicted to his cell phone and easily distracted, was just about the easiest target he had ever faced.

"You will stay right here in orbit. No matter what happens until I return."

"I will stay right here in orbit," the Captain replied, his tone dead, his eyes half-closed.

"Exactly," Floyd said. "And when I do return, you will be prepared and waiting to go immediately into your highest warp setting."

"Highest warp setting." The Captain's pupils were huge, and he was swaying from side to side.

"In fact," Floyd continued, "if you never even consider leaving until I get back then there will be a million extra credits for you when we return to Arcturis City."

That last part was a lie, but the subconscious wants what the subconscious wants and if the Captain was convinced on a deep level that staying was in his best interest then stay he would. Of course, he wouldn't remember any of this afterward and even if he did, "considering" something is awfully hard to prove in court, so there would be no pay-out. It was simply extra insurance toward Floyd's continued survival. He released the Captain from his spell.

"To the mission!" Floyd said and pulled out his portal.

"To the mission," the Captain parroted back and raised a salute.

Sometimes it was just too easy.

Floyd stepped through the portal and onto Regulus. He looked around and checked his watch, relieved to find he was early. He double checked that the small orb in his suitcase was still there and intact. It was the gizmo that was going to cause Soda problems. And it was snuggled safely in his briefcase.

Floyd had nothing left to do but find a nearby shop to hang out in until everything went crazy. Ground zero. It was sort of fun looking around at all the locals who had no idea what was going to hit them. The calm before the storm felt electric to him, almost like he was hunting.

He entered a generic looking coffee shop, approached the counter, and passed a young woman who was holding a coffee cup in visibly trembling hands. "Careful, miss. Maybe you should switch to decaf."

"Bite me, generic business guy," the woman replied.

Rude. *This planet deserves whatever it gets.*

He ordered coffee and a small Danish and sat down to play his phone game until he heard the beginnings of the inevitable chaos.

* * *

ARI AWOKE IN PAIN. Initially, she thought she was seeing double; then she realized that the creature caring for her had a fin on his head and two sets of arms. Carpe. It was a startling way to regain consciousness.

"Is she okay?"

Ari turned her head slightly and saw Fleek kneeling down. A sharp pain gripped her head, followed by a wave of nausea.

"I think so," said Carpe.

"Where's Kracken?" Ari waited for the answer instead of trying to move her head again.

"He left. Took our portal. I heard you talking, and I came around the corner in time for your big reveal about him being a spy. It's a good thing too. You cleverly got him to confess, since he wasn't saying anything and from my vantage point I couldn't see the gun. I would have never known you were in trouble."

Ari tried to process what he was saying. "Yeah, I'm clever like that. Blurt everything out. It's a great plan. Works every time."

"Do you remember anything?" Carpe asked her.

"I think so," answered Ari "Why?"

"Because before he knocked you out, you were going on and on about some plan and how we didn't have much time."

Ari tried to think. *That sounds like me.* She remembered

arguing with Kracken and losing consciousness, but nothing before that. What had she been doing? Her computer. The thought was there, but it wasn't connecting to anything else.

"Get me to my computer."

Fleek and Carpe each gently took an arm and helped her up and over to the keypad. Another wave of pain and nausea washed over her and she nearly blacked out again. "Hey, do you guys have anything for the pain? It's distracting, and I'm going to need to concentrate."

"You watch her," Fleek said. "I'll be right back."

Ari read her search history looking for clues that might jog her memory and looked at the local news feed. Nothing. She looked at the console with the view of the planet's capital city. Chaos. Then she looked back at the news feed. Still nothing.

Fleek returned with the little bag containing the Blue Pixie. Warning signs began going off in Ari's brain. These kinds of drugs were not her style, but at this point, she had little choice.

"Look," Fleek said, "pour this directly onto your tongue, it's like pixie sticks. Your mental clarity will come right back and trust me you will feel no pain."

Ari was dubious, but there was too much on the line and no time. "How much? Is there a measuring utensil or something in the baggie?"

Fleek rolled his eyes, grabbed the bag, and mimed for her to stick out her tongue. He poured the powder.

Ok, just a little bit more than a coating of the tongue, thought Ari. Looked like a tablespoon or so. She wondered how long the Blue Pixie would take to hit her.

It wasn't long.

"Wow," she said, noting that it even tasted like pixie sticks, something she wasn't expecting. "That was fast. What about side effects?"

"I wouldn't worry about that," Fleek said.

"Why not?" Ari asked.

"Because," he said, looking at what was happening on the planet on the console, "we'll probably all be dead soon, anyway. Have fun. Good luck." Then he turned to leave with Carpe and his other band mates.

"Wait. I can't do it alone. I need, um, Carpe."

Fleek nodded, and Carpe came back and knelt next to Ari.

"Ok," Fleek said, "but we're going to need him back soon."

Ari had recovered some of her train of thought and was typing furiously. Not only was everything coming back to her, she was flying past where she thought her research idea had been going.

Again, she would have to hurry, but the prospects were intriguing. She soon reached a point where her extremities started tingling. Or maybe that was the Pixie stuff. She stopped typing and watched the local news feed. Still nothing. She studied the console. Chaos. Weird. There had to be some communications barrier on the planet keeping messages from leaving. That's probably how Soda had got away with it, making sure nobody knew what was going on.

"Alright, Ari. What's the plan?" Carpe asked. "Whoa, your pupils are super dilated."

"We have to get onto the surface of the planet. Wait. Did you say Kracken went through the portal?"

"Aye."

"Why would he do that? Did you find out anything from him? Is he a double agent?"

"The only thing I found out was that he was concealing a blade." Carpe twisted his body to show a shallow stab on his torso. It was still bleeding. "It's the only reason he got away."

"Alright," said Ari, wincing at the wound in sympathy, "I guess we can use a temporary portal through the ship. It'll get us there, but it won't get us back. If we survive, we'll have to be picked up."

She tapped into the ship's portal interface. "How long has Kracken been gone?"

"Ten or fifteen minutes, give or take."

"Well, if he was a spy, we can assume he knows about everything. Me, Kirian. Our plan."

"Fleek and the song." Carpe added.

Ari stared at him like he had a horn growing out of his forehead.

"Look," she said, "I don't mean to put down your art or anything, and it would be great if the Overseer likes the music enough or cares what people think enough not to destroy us, but I doubt it. And I'm not counting on it. Sorry."

"Don't be," Carpe replied.

"Good. If I'm right with these calculations, then this planet has odd properties that could amplify the Temporarily Physical Holographic Weapon's power."

"I know what TPHWs are," Carpe answered, looking wounded that she would spell it out for him.

"How? If it's illegal, experimental, and only the Overseer has any control over them, how could you possibly know about them?"

"Trust me, the illegal, experimental, and highly dangerous community is a tiny and nosy one."

"Ok," said Ari, "moving on. Kirian's going to need all the help she can get." She got up and made her way toward the temporary, non-portable portal, then staggered. Carpe caught her and helped her through.

* * *

ARI EMERGED on the other side. She had seen in general what was going on via the console, but she'd had the volume turned way down so she could concentrate.

Seeing it through the console interface in no way conveyed the chaos she heard and saw around her. The Overseer was an evil piece of work. Ari was beginning to regret nothing in defying Soda, even if it killed her, and it probably would.

She turned in a circle to get a better sense of what was going on around her. As expected, the TPHW was spitting out dozens of creatures at a time. Too many for even Kirian to handle.

And if she was right, the holographic weapons would be able to last even longer on this planet due to its unusual properties.

There was something else, what was it?

It was very hard to concentrate with all of the screaming. Kracken. Where had he got to?

"Hey Carpe, keep an eye out for Kracken. He could be trouble."

Ari could see a swarm of drones buzzing around Kirian. Kirian's Stingr cut down two of the drones. Three more took their place. Ari balled a fist. Wasn't it enough to kill her? The Overseer was filming the whole thing too?

Focus, Ari.

"Carpe, we need to find the nearest television station as soon as possible."

She and Carpe had to duck behind some vehicles to avoid a stray rampaging TPHW creature that had broken away from Kirian. Ari couldn't help but peek. This batch looked like upright, walking, short-haired dogs. *Amazing,* thought Ari, *they look so real.*

"Television station?" Carpe asked. "Kracken must have hit you in the head harder than I thought."

Chapter 24

Ari and Carpe scanned the skyline for the tell-tale call letters and slogan. Then she saw it, off to the right, only a block away.

'EHDG' one of the signs proudly announced, 'Entertainment with an edge.'

"Over there," she shouted and ran toward it.

The television station building looked deserted. Ari snuck another look at Kirian. The advancing hordes were not just threatening her; they were beginning to get past her into the city at large. Kirian was working hard, though, slashing in all directions, Stingrs in both hands.

"Hold on, Kirian!" She yelled even though she knew Kirian couldn't hear her.

Ari ducked into the building with Carpe right behind and found the obligatory directory. She consulted it.

"Fourth floor," she announced.

A tremor hit. At least Ari hoped it was a tremor and not a side effect of the drugs she had taken, but then she saw Carpe sway as well.

He leaned a hand against a wall to steady himself. "Better take the stairs," he said. "I can't believe this place still has electricity."

"Good point," Ari said and pulled out a flashlight just in case.

"Hey, what are we looking for once we get up there?"

"Equipment."

"That narrows it down."

"I don't know yet, I'll have to see it to know if it'll work," she answered. "Grab everything, turn it on, bring it to me. We'll have to figure it out through trial and error."

It was a helpful thing that chaos reigned outside because the studio was deserted, leaving them to do what they needed to do. Or so Ari thought.

"You're not authorized to be here," a new voice chimed in.

A tall, string-bean looking guy emerged from the shadows. A name tag identified him as Lrrrje Krennnlis, President of the Studio. The name tag was a paper, temporary one. It struck Ari as odd because none of the television station presidents she had ever met had worn name tags, much less paper ones with sticky tape on the back.

Ari was in no mood for the interruption. "Look, Lrrrje, in case you haven't noticed, your city is under attack. We're trying to help."

Carpe kept an eye on Lrrrje as Ari continued to poke around, looking into nearby rooms for the equipment she needed.

"No," Lrrrje said, pointing through a large window off to the side, "she's trying to help, you're trying to steal our equipment."

Ari realized with a jolt that he was pointing at Kirian, clearly visible through the window. Although outnumbered, she was still fighting. Ari ran to the window. Kirian looked winded and was bleeding from various wounds on her arms and legs.

"Ari," said Carpe, "you have to find what you came here for. It's the only way to help her."

"And look, you, string bean," he said. "I don't believe that little sticky tag makes you president of anything. And it certainly won't keep me from snapping you in half. Besides," he pointed out the window, "we're with her. You think she's going to last much longer? Do you think she'll be able to save this whole planet by herself?"

Ari turned to see what string bean would do.

"Fine, I'm not the president," he said, his expression having changed after taking a good look at Carpe and hearing the whole snap-you-in-half half thing.

"It's just that this is the best job I ever had. I'm part of something, you know? And I was hoping that when, I mean if this whole thing blows over..."

A distant explosion made the building sway and groan.

"Well, I was just hoping it could all go back to normal."

"Look, Lrrrje," Ari said, "we're honestly with her. We're trying to help. Do you want to save this place? Then help us."

"Help you steal the studio's equipment?" He was dubious. "How in stars is that going to help her or my city?"

"The string bean has a good point," said Carpe.

Lrrrje opened his mouth and started to object to being called a string bean.

"Save it," Carpe said, holding a hand up to silence him. "Help us, stay out of our way, or 'snap.'" He pantomimed the snapping with his hands.

"I don't like him," Lrrrje told Ari.

"You get used to him. Look, we don't have time for this. We need a special kind of camera, one that can see and manipulate electromagnetic frequencies."

"That's a very expensive camera."

Ari turned toward him. "Where is it, Lrrrje?"

Carpe advanced on him fast, losing patience.

"I'll help you," he said to Ari. "Just call him off."

"Show us where the stupid camera is, Lrrrje," Ari said.

"Ok, but I don't think it will help."

"Why not?" Carpe asked.

"Because only the real Studio President can authorize entry into that area."

"Show us, now!" Ari yelled.

Reluctantly, and muttering to himself the whole way, Lrrrje led them through a series of hallways. Finally, he showed them into an inner room that had expensive looking cameras that were locked in glass cases. He pointed at the middle one, and exactly what Ari needed was right there.

"I don't have the code, though," Lrrrje said, "and the glass is bullet proofed and heat resistant."

Ari dug the Stingr Kirian had given her out of her pocket. It sprang to life. The sheer beauty of it amazed her. It shimmered and sparkled and hummed, taking on a life of its own.

The blade itself was tiny, sheer, almost delicate looking, but she could feel the hum of its power all the way down to her toes. This thing was the real deal. She swung it a little, left to right. She did it partially to feel what it was like and partially to get a better feel for what Kirian was going through outside.

Lrrrje screamed and Carpe shouted. They were way too close to feel safe.

"Stop that!" Carpe yelled. "Are you crazy?"

"Probably," said Ari, and brought the full force of the Stingr down against the glass case holding the camera she needed. She figured the case wasn't designed against this weapon. She was right. The glass crashed around them. Ari turned off the Stinger, and tried to put it back into her pocket, but it was hot. She dropped it onto the floor with a clattering noise.

"And I thought you were the dangerous one," Lrrrje said to Carpe.

"Aye," Carpe answered, "it's always the innocent looking ones you have to watch out for."

Ari picked her way through the glass to the camera. It was heavier than she expected it to be. It was made of real metal, and all of the dials were sturdy and precise. She picked her way back out of the glass carefully and handed the camera to Carpe. Then she retrieved the Stingr from the floor, no way she was leaving something that awesome behind. This time it was cool enough to place back into her jeans pocket.

"Hey," said Lrrrje to Ari, "use the camera strap, that thing is expensive, and you don't want to break it!"

Ari hated to admit it, but he was right. "But if I use the strap, I'll look like a tourist."

"Ok," said Carpe, "enough of this. Ari, do you need anything else?"

Ari smiled. "I think this will do. Now we just need some extra batteries."

"Follow me," Lrrrje called and led the way down the hall. They secured the extra batteries and headed back down to the lobby area.

"Now what?" Carpe asked.

"Let's go give it a try," Ari said.

Lrrrje balked. "You're not honestly thinking of going out there, are you?"

The building shook again. "Just get us back to the lobby, Lrrrje."

He led them back to where they had entered. They looked outside the glass doors and could see the chaos right outside.

"You ready?" Carpe asked.

Ari nodded, and they emptied out onto the street. Lrrrje followed them outside.

The noise hit them immediately. It was hard to know which way to turn. From the upper floors inside, it had been easier to see everything. Kirian and the hordes of TPHWs had been clearly visible. Now they were obscured by buildings and smoke.

Ari coughed from the smoke. It was probably best to get out of the immediate vicinity. They had to get moving anyway. Just as soon as they got their bearings. "We have to get closer to Kirian."

"Closer? To the battle? Are you crazy?" asked Lrrrje.

"What part of this whole battle thing don't you get? We said we were going to help Kirian." Ari was getting annoyed. "If you don't want to help, why don't you just go back and huddle in the building or something."

She turned her back to Lrrrje and faced Carpe to formulate a plan. Then a Stingr appeared and hovered perilously close to her throat.

* * *

TRISHA WANDERED around Main Street on Regulus looking for the coffee shop Brad had suggested. She wondered if he knew just how much she needed the coffee.

She found the place and ordered a double expresso. Anything to keep her awake until Brad arrived. She looked around and didn't see him. Where could he be?

She sat down and began to sip the coffee, keeping an eye on the front door. A balding guy in a boring suit and briefcase passed.

"Careful miss," he said, looking at her, "maybe you should switch to decaf."

Rage grew inside of her. "Bite me, generic business suit guy," she said.

How dare he? She glared at him, and he kept moving. She was still seething when Brad arrived.

"There you are," she said testily.

"Sorry," he said. "It's harder for me to get around. I'm on an awful lot of no-fly lists."

That made sense.

Luckily for her, she was a well-respected journalism student on the planet solely for research purposes and didn't have such problems.

"Did you know your hands are shaking?" he asked.

Trisha looked down at her hands and set the half full coffee cup on the table.

"Never mind that. Look," she said, "I've been up almost twenty-four hours doing research. I need everything you know about whatever this is so I can finish my thesis, leave, and go to sleep, okay?"

"Well, I don't know how much you know about the subject. Where should I start?" Brad asked.

"Assume I know nothing," Trisha said, turning on the recording device, "and tell me everything."

Brad told her everything. And Trisha was very grateful for the recording device because she only caught bits and pieces of the narrative while trying very hard not to nod off.

He talked about TMPHs or some weird monster generator thing that the Octopus Overlord supposedly used to distract from illegal mining activities and planetary destruction. Something like that, anyway. The most important thing to her was that the more he talked, the more confident she was that the whole thing was bollocks and she'd be out of there in a few hours with a funny story and enough points to finish her thesis.

Her confidence faltered at the sound of the first explosion.

Chapter 25

"You guys ready?" Fleek asked.

He knew they were because it was time. The studio was ready. The equipment was ready. The avatar software was up and running and tested. The only thing left was to set up the camera.

"Has anyone seen the camera?" Fleek asked.

"Here it is," said Marco, after a few minutes of rummaging. "We only have one problem."

"What's that?" Fleek asked.

"No Carpe."

Suddenly, the space ship went completely dark. "Ok," said Marco, "two problems."

"What happened to the power?" Fleek asked the darkness and Marco.

Neither answered.

A total power outage had never happened before. Usually, backup power came on immediately, but not in this case.

Fleek's first thought was to go to the console and bring up the manual. He only had to bump into the first wall before he figured out what was wrong with that plan. No lights meant no electricity which meant no console.

"How do you get your power, anyway?" Marco asked.

"Same way everybody does," he answered, "I pay my bill every month."

“Sucker.” Marco smiled. Fleek knew this because several of his teeth glowed in the dark. Fleek was jealous. If he survived the night, he planned to schedule a visit to the dentist ASAP.

"There are other ways to light a ship, mate." The glow in the dark teeth were speaking hope.

"You do that,” Fleek said. “I'll get Carpe back."

"Deal."

* * *

EVEN THOUGH IT was a thin blade, Ari could still feel its heat near her throat. She knew how lethal it was. When Carpe's eyes bulged, she knew it was a really bad situation. Carpe held his four hands in the air. One of them still held the camera. His eye twitched, and his mouth tightened.

"What are you doing, Lrrrje?" Ari asked. Anger rose inside her. He must have picked her pocket. The light particles in the Stingr buzzed with energy and heat.

"Don't you want me to help save this city? This television station? How's hurting me going to help anything?"

Keeping one eye on Carpe, Lrrrje tilted his head to the side and moved her to the right, where Ari saw her wanted poster on the side of the building.

Ugh. Why did they have to use the picture from the office party three years ago? Even her work badge photo would have been better. *Figures*.

"The reward for you will pay for my own television station."

Ari exhaled. What was the universe coming to? No loyalty, no morals. In the end, everything just came down to money.

Lrrrje stepped closer and got a tight grip on her upper arm. It wasn't hard because he was so tall. He held the sword at her throat between himself and Carpe and began to drag Ari backward.

"No. Lrrrje. You don't know what you're doing," Ari pleaded. "I have to help Kirian. Nobody else can!"

Carpe's communicator buzzed.

"Hey, Carpe," Fleek said. "We need you back here. It's show time."

Lrrrje looked at Carpe.

"I'm a little busy right now, Fleek."

"It's time to play the song, Carpe. Get back on the ship," Fleek insisted.

"Ari needs me right now. Can't leave yet."

Ari considered Carpe. He was the one person on the ship she had been most skeptical of, based on appearance and background. Kracken had betrayed them, and Lrrrje wanted the money. But when it mattered, Carpe was sticking by her. Even with his new career on the line.

Carpe stood still, holding the electromagnetic camera high over his head, unwilling to put it down even though his hands were up.

She got an idea.

String bean wasn't a humanoid life form. He would be subject to a different set of harmful parameters for electromagnetic energy than humans.

Ari glanced at the gun in Carpe's hand and then back to his face.

Lrrrje, tall as he was, had to reach his arm down against her chest to pull her back. It was effective except for the fact that it left her hands free.

She held out three fingers as secretly as she could. Carpe gave an almost imperceptible nod. Then she held out two fingers, six, and eight. Based on what she could remember from her research of Lrrrje's species grouping, that would be the most dangerous frequency for string bean, while probably leaving her and Carpe okay.

Probably.

Lrrrje continued dragging her backward. They were inside the building now. The light sword dangled. Lrrrje got careless, and it brushed against her shoulder, making a hole in her t-shirt and slicing into skin. Blood flowed down her arm.

"Owwww. What is wrong with you?" Ari yelled.

Lrrrje turned her around so that they were facing each other.

"You're a lot of trouble," he said. "And the flyer did say dead or alive."

Ari tried to back up since he had released her, but she had nowhere to go. Her back was literally against the wall.

Carpe burst through the entrance door, brandishing the camera.

"What do you think that's going to do?" Lrrrje asked derisively. He didn't even have the decency to be afraid.

Without a word, Carpe raised the camera and hit the button. A pale-blue light ray shot forward from the lens. It hit Lrrrje in the chest.

Lrrrje collapsed to his knees, mouth open, screaming in agony. Carpe continued firing and advancing until he was right on top of Lrrrje. He set the camera down and then snapped string bean in half.

Ari wasn't quite expecting that. She was grateful for his quick thinking and help, but was also quite certain she'd never forget the noise of Lrrrje's crunching bones.

Carpe turned to her. "How'd you do that?"

"What?" Ari asked.

"Figure out how to turn the camera into a gun?"

"Oh." Ari smiled. "Up in the director's office, I reversed the flow in the settings. It's completely experimental. Normally the camera pulls the images around it inward. I made the energy flow outward. Had no idea it would work. Thanks for saving me. We make a pretty good team."

She took a final look at Lrrrje, shuddered, and retrieved the electromagnetic camera and the Stingr.

"Okay," he answered. "I guess you're right, we do make a good team."

"Last chance, Carpe," Fleek said over the communicator. He sounded mad. "We need you, man. Can you get to the coordinates I'm sending you?"

"I gotta do this," Carpe said to Ari. Then he pushed the button on his communicator. "I'm on my way, Fleek. Good luck, Ari." He winked at her and then was gone.

Ari took the camera and headed outside. The first test had been a success. Would the rest of her plan fare as well?

A nearby yell from Kirian made Ari sprint toward the sound. The one thing for sure was that whatever was happening so far in this city, it was aimed at Kirian.

* * *

WHEN FLEEK RETURNED WITH CARPE, the two of them made their way back to the studio using communicator flashlights. As they entered the room, the power returned, and everything came back on. Sort of.

Before the power failure, the lighting had given a semi-drab, poorly-lit ambiance, but the light was now blinding like the sun. They groaned and covered their eyes to give themselves time to adjust.

"What did you do?" Fleek asked Marco, who he hoped was nearby and could hear him.

"Let's just say that it's extremely illegal, but from now on you'll have no problems running your coffee pot."

After a couple of minutes, their eyes adjusted, their equipment was ready, their sparkling avatars were perfect, and they were on stage ready to go.

"Ok guys," said Fleek, settling in at his keyboard with the television camera remote in his hand. "Are you ready to make history by breaking every broadcast law, noise code violation, and music industry regulations in the galaxy? Are you ready to rocket us to Pirate Radio Stardom?"

The band cheered.

He hit the button to go live. The camera started recording, and the band started playing. The most expensive, state-of-the-art, not yet legal, amplified boosters that billions of units of hacked currency had bought, kicked into gear.

"We are Chemical Zombies," Fleek screamed. "And this lame galaxy has been waiting a long time for a song this great, so here goes. Oh yeah, and we'd like to dedicate this song to Kirian, Destroyer of Planets."

Fleek gave himself fully to the music, to the song, to the fractal math that had led his whole life to this moment. To fame and fortune and groupies.

Rock and roll.

Chapter 26

Drexyl scanned the room. The console was on, and Soda stood in front of it, staring at the images playing on the screen. He jumped up and rushed to her side.

Kirian was on the screen battling a new wave of TPHWs. A battle she was on the verge of losing.

"Why is Kirian up there again so soon? She should have had the requisite seventy-two hours to rest and plan and—"

"I changed the rules," Soda said, turning to him savagely. "They're my rules. My servants. I do whatever I want, and nobody can stop me."

Drexyl stared at Soda, who was concentrating, fixated on the screen. She had one tentacle over her head, three in front of the screen, and one on each side of her in a strange, fixed position. Like she was trying to be a television antenna.

"What are you doing to her?" he demanded.

"I'm going to kill her. And I wanted you to see it. Thank goodness you woke up in time," she said without moving or breaking eye contact.

"Stop it!" he pleaded.

He had no power, and neither did Kirian. All he could do was watch the screen. Soda leaned forward, and Kirian dropped to her knees, the lights in her hair brightened and then went out.

"No. I'll do anything, Soda. Don't kill her, please."

"Oh, this is happening," she answered. "And why all of this anger? This fear? You think this woman cares about you? She doesn't. You're just another Overseer minion to her. Somebody who orders her around. Someone who works for me. Name one reason she would care about you?"

Drexyl froze.

Soda was right. How could Kirian possibly know how he felt about her? He'd never told her. He couldn't. Not in front of Soda.

His world since captivity had been Soda and the Celestials. Soda and Kirian. Kirian had fascinated him since the first time he saw her.

The creatures on the screen charged at Kirian. She was going to die. Right there on the screen. Right in front of him. It was too much for him to take. With a scream he charged Soda, knocking her down and breaking her concentration.

Taken by surprise, her tentacles splayed. Her wobbly head with eyes huge in surprise bulged before she hit the floor. From that moment on, everything seemed to slow into a strange, out of time experience.

* * *

AFTER LISTENING to Brad's explanation of what might happen, Trisha expected the explosions to begin downtown, where they already were, but that wasn't the case. The first explosion came from the opposite direction.

"Come on," Brad said, "I have a rental car."

Explosion chasing. That woke Trisha up a little. This was what she hoped journalism would be like, chasing actual events and not just conspiracy theories. She was pretty sure whatever this distant disruption turned out to be, it probably wasn't conspiracy theory related because she had heard it with her own ears. She jumped into his car, and they sped off.

Trisha, in the passenger's seat, texted her friend Jen to let her know what kind of adventure she was having. It took a couple of minutes to figure out exactly how to word the particular text, though, and by the time she hit send they had reached the vicinity of the explosion.

Brad hit the brakes, and the car screeched to a halt. The smoke was several blocks away, but close enough to smell once they got out of the car. Trisha checked her phone for a reply. Nothing. A message told her the text had not sent.

Weird.

Brad led the way toward the smoke. People were running past them, fleeing the area. Trisha stopped one. "What's going on?"

"Gas leak. They're evacuating the area," the person said before scampering off.

Men in uniforms worked machinery near the smoke. Trisha had covered local gas leaks on her planet, and this was not normally how things went down.

Usually, fire crews evacuated everybody, shut off the gas main, which took a while, and then they usually brought in the rest of the crew.

If the explosion was from a gas leak then why were there workers in uniform digging in the earth at the site of the blast? She and Brad exchanged a nervous glance and continued toward the commotion instead of away from it.

As they drew close, an armed guard held up his hand. "You people are supposed to be evacuating."

"What's going on?" Trisha demanded.

"A gas leak, lady. Now beat it."

"Who uses armed guards to keep people away from a gas leak?" Brad asked. "Why aren't you and your men evacuating, then?"

"Because we're fixing it, aren't we?"

The man was getting mad, and a vein popped out on his forehead. He kept looking nervously around at the other workers and the machinery in motion. "I'm telling you for the last time to get out of here."

Trisha held her phone up and zoomed in on the machinery in time to record a chunk of earth and metal being thrown out of the hole onto the ground nearby. Several men in the same uniform as the guard collected the hunk of rock.

The guard saw Trisha recording the video and pointed his weapon at her.

"Let it go, Ken," one of the workers behind him said, "leave 'em. We're almost done here anyway."

Ken turned and joined the rest of the crew. Brad and Trisha stood still wondering what to do next. The men were leaving the site, and the place was emptying out fast.

Neither had the time to think about what to do next. A series of ground rocking explosions, much louder and stronger than before, turned a piece of downtown behind them into a pile of smoldering rubble.

Trisha turned toward it and frowned. Enough of Brad's crazy conspiracy theory had bled into her consciousness to know that things were turning bad fast. Brad's face drained of color.

"What's the matter, Brad? You're the one who knows about all of this stuff, right? Haven't you been through this before? What do we do now?"

He shook his head. "I know the stories, I've seen anecdotal evidence, but I've never been on the planet for an actual event. Because usually, these on-planet events end with..."

He didn't finish.

"With planetary deletion," Trisha finished the thought for him, hoping he was wrong. She rechecked her phone. No messages were getting in or out.

Crap.

She wished she was still back at the dorm studying.

* * *

KIRIAN SWUNG WILDLY, a light sword in each hand. Sweat poured off of her body from the effort.

She felt the pain from several wounds, and a trickle of blood ran down her left leg. There was never a break from the humming of regeneration, and the incessant flow of opponents.

This was it. She was going to die live and on television. *Thus passes Kirian, Destroyer of Planets.*

"Hey, are you people getting this?" she taunted. "Do I have the high score yet?"

It wasn't just the TPHWs either; there was something else, she could feel it. A presence, maybe.

If she had her normal break between waves between opponents, she could have figured it out. Maybe. Or at least identified it. But there was barely time to breathe and bleed, and she was doing plenty of both.

The one good thing, despite the increased size and number of her opponents, is that they didn't seem any smarter. If anything, it was quite the opposite. They milled more than they attacked, approaching randomly and slowly. It was only a problem when they grew too numerous and surrounded her, stepping forward to slash when her back was turned.

Kirian could feel...her? The Overseer?

A voice broke through the background noise.

"Kirian," it said. "Time to die."

In the past, the creatures had howled when they attacked, but in all her years as a Celestial, none had ever spoken.

"Soda is that you? What in stars name are you doing here?"

Kirian knew the Overseer was located on the capital planet surrounded by security in a secret location. None of this made any sense.

"Foolish being. I have powers beyond your wildest dreams. Nobody in this galaxy compares to me."

* * *

ARI MOVED close enough to Kirian and the battle to see the dog-looking TPHWs spilling out. She fired a test shot and hit two of them in the chest with a purple stream. They slowed and flickered, but it didn't stop them. It disrupted the field the TPHW creatures were using. The camera worked—at least in part.

Fleek's voice thundered around her, and the Chemical Zombies played The Song.

Great, she thought, the live-streamed end of my life will have a rock soundtrack.

Her idea was sound. The camera weapon had disrupted the TPHW field, but it wasn't enough. She had a nagging idea though, about the electromagnetic field. Was there another frequency that would be more effective?

In theory, it would be like a master electromagnetic key. She searched the camera's electromagnetic options, but still wasn't sure.

When she looked up again, the TPHWs were parting as a tentacled monster materialized in front of her and Kirian. It appeared to be the Overseer herself. Not possible.

How can she be here?

"I came to kill you myself," the Octopus Overseer said to Kirian. She slithered forward through the horde of manufactured creatures and paused. "Ugh, what is this awful music? I'll take care of that after I take care of you, Kirian."

Ari aimed the camera at the Overseer and fired.

Soda laughed and turned to her, waving a tentacle. A blast of wind hit Ari and threw her backward down the street. She dropped the camera.

Ari looked up to see Soda advancing on Kirian. Without touching her, without even making physical contact, just by gesturing, Soda picked Kirian up and lifted her three feet into the air. Kirian's arms reached up to her throat, gasping for breath, struggling against the unseen force.

Ari got up and lunged for the camera.

Soda glanced back and then let her. "Your light ray can't hurt me, dear. And don't worry; you're next."

* * *

DREXYL EXPECTED Soda to rage at him. To kill him. Something. Instead, she got back up, shot him a wicked smile, and refocused on the console.

Drexyl watched her move into an entirely different configuration of angles, tentacles, and body placement.

"Watch this," she said.

Ari ran into the picture. What was she doing there? She had something in her hand. A camera?

Ari pointed it and fired. The TPHW she hit with the beam of light flickered.

For a moment, he dared to hope. Then, on the screen, Soda materialized in front of Ari.

Drexyl swiveled his gaze from Soda here in the room, to the screen, and then back.

Soda was concentrating again, eyes closed, tentacles stiff with exertion. She appeared in both places at once. And on the screen, she was approaching Kirian.

What was going on?

* * *

THE SEVERAL MINUTES it took for Brad to drive them downtown gave Trisha time to consider the reckless, sleep-deprived choices she had been making recently. She wanted a do-over and very much hoped that when they got to the source of this new disruption, it was something mundane. Like an interstellar attack or a slumbering monster awakened by a brand-new energy accelerator.

Brad brought the car to a screeching halt just outside of the chaos zone. It was close enough to see but far enough away to stave off, at least temporarily, any real collateral damage.

Now that they had a view, they could see a wild-looking girl wielding double light swords and battling what looked like very large, badly done CGI walking dogs.

“Ok,” Trisha said, “help me out, what am I looking at here?”

"I see what appears to be TPHWs and possibly a Celestial." He zoomed in on the girl with his camera. "Oh no, it looks like Kirian, Destroyer of Planets. What do you think? Should we help her?"

"Help her?" Trisha asked, still not believing her eyes and trying to figure out if she was hallucinating.

"So those dog-looking things are the weapons generated by the Octopus Overlord?"

"Yes, that’s right. Cool, eh?"

"She can just make them out of thin air?"

"That's the consensus."

"Wait, according to you guys, the Celestials are her warriors. Right?"

"Yes again. I gotta say, I didn't think you were paying that much attention earlier, but you were getting the gist of it."

"So why is the Neon Octopus Overlord attacking her own warrior? It doesn't make sense."

"Oh yeah," said Brad. "You've got a point."

They sat in the car for a few moments, watching the situation unfold. Try as she might, Trisha couldn’t think of a plan.

If this planet was going to be destroyed and it was all going to end soon anyway, she wasn't sure why she should bother getting out of the car.

Then, a giant Praying Mantis ran by. It had a bloody arm in its mouth and a briefcase in one hand. Trisha locked her car door; then she started hyperventilating. Brad screamed like a girl.

"You saw that, right?" Trish asked between ragged breaths. Maybe he didn't see it. Maybe it wasn't real.

Brad stopped screaming long enough to answer. "The Praying Mantis with the, um, briefcase? Y-Yes."

"Is that related to the TPHSs or the warrior girl or whatever?"

"Never heard of one of those," Brad answered, his voice deeper than usual, probably overcompensating for the earlier screaming.

Trisha was inclined to stay in the car before that thing ran by, she certainly wasn't going to risk getting out now.

As if the events weren't surreal enough, rock music started playing. Actually, it started with a male voice introducing the band. They called themselves Chemical Zombies and then music exploded through the atmosphere. It was ear-shatteringly loud, and if not for the possible gas leak, hordes of giant dog TPHWs, explosions, and the Praying Mantis to worry about, Trisha would have probably complained to the proper authorities about the music's volume.

"What in bloody stars is going on now?" Trisha shouted, trying to be heard above the music.

Brad didn't answer. The two of them sat in the car listening. "Do all planetary destructions get a soundtrack or just us? Because frankly, despite being way too loud, I kind of like it."

"Yeah, me too."

Some light blasts added to the confrontation, but Trish and Brad were far enough away not to get hit by any stray shots.

"Looks to me like a tourist blasting things with a television camera," Trisha said, hoping that matched what Brad was seeing.

"Yup," he answered.

A meteor rocketed down in a spectacular plume of light and smoke and hit the tourist with the camera smack in the face.

"Ooooohh," they reacted together.

"Did you see that?" Brad yelled over the music. "Brutal."

"I mean, what are the odds of that happening while everything else is going on?" Trisha asked.

"Hey, look at that, she got back up," Brad said, "good for her. Too bad the planet's about to explode, though. But hey, she's a feisty one."

Continuing to watch the scene like television commentators, Trisha wished she had a snack. Then something appeared in the middle of the dogs.

"What's that?" Trisha asked.

"What?" Brad asked. He had been zoning out in the other direction.

"Look," Trisha shouted, "what does that look like to you?"

"It can't be," Brad said. "The Neon Octopus Overlord?"

* * *

FLOYD HAD RUN through the circuit of his favorite phone games several times when the first downtown explosions shook the windows and the surrounding buildings.

Finally.

He was getting seriously bored.

Frightened patrons inside of the coffee shop first huddled and then left to find cover or go home. Floyd relaxed. He had a few minutes to spare. Soon it was just him, the cook, and a single barista looking over the place.

All this waiting made him hungry. Dare he transform here? Why not? These people were all doomed anyway.

The decision made, he twitched and changed into his true, hungry self. Much to his delight, their screams mixed in nicely with those coming from nearby downtown. In the confusion, he didn't attract any attention, not that it mattered.

Several minutes later, satiated and feeling oodles better, he checked his watch. *Oops, I'm late*. He grabbed his briefcase and headed out the door.

"Easy peasy." Those were the exact words the clerk at the Technical Gizmo store used to describe how easy the orb was to use. "You simply get within a twelve-block radius of the area you want to unblock and you throw it high into the air," he had said. "And then it explodes, destroying any communications-blocking signals in the atmosphere."

Floyd ran through the streets in the general direction of the melee. At one point, he got close enough to see the Celestial the Overseer had sent here. It was Kirian.

Huh. Bummer for her. She was surrounded by the typical TPHW dogs that the Overseer preferred.

He found a good general location to throw the orb and stopped. Hopefully, this would be the end of the hard-core work he would have to do. He threw it high in the air watching it go. At its zenith, it emitted a loud pop.

Floyd stood underneath it, wondering what would happen next. He squinted up to see if it would fall back down, but it had vanished. A meteor shot off toward his right. He shielded his face from the light with his arm. Huh, what are the odds?

Then he scurried away, spitting out the arm he'd forgotten he still had in his mouth before entering his portable portal.

Oh dear. How embarrassing to have run through the city streets with something in his teeth.

* * *

ARI LOOKED AT KIRIAN, who was fading fast into unconsciousness in Soda's grip. There was only one chance. She switched the setting on the camera and changed the frequency. This time to 4747.

Here goes nothing.

She aimed at Soda and fired.

All of the TPHW's exploded and, as fate would have it, to the rhythm of the song.

Soda dropped Kirian and turned toward Ari, her face quivering with rage.

"You have no idea what you've done," Soda hissed.

Kirian lay on the ground, gasping for air.

"You can't stop me from killing her, Ari."

Yes I can. Ari raised the camera and fired again. This time the beam of light hit Soda in her center of mass instead of the chest like before.

Soda turned to face Ari, eyes wide in surprise. Then there was a loud pop.

At first, Ari wasn't sure if the sound was from the song, the camera, or Soda. Something else off to her left popped.

She turned toward the noise and saw a giant Praying Mantis running away. She screamed and the hair on the back of her neck prickled. And then it was gone.

Ari turned back toward Kirian, but all she saw was a very bright light. And then nothing at all.

* * *

DREXYL WATCHED in horror as the Soda on the planet somehow picked Kirian up by the throat without even touching her.

He could see the Soda at his side concentrating, miming the choking movements with her tentacle here in the room.

On the screen, Ari tried to shoot her with the camera weapon and failed. Then Ari picked up the camera and fired again.

The Soda on the planet flickered and twitched. The Soda in the room with him flinched and trembled. Drexyl kept glancing back and forth trying to find a connection. He couldn't believe what he was seeing. The thoughts in his mind raced faster than he could follow.

Here in the room, Soda had fallen onto her side. She lay in a trembling, quivering heap. It didn't take long for her to recover, though.

Drexyl looked to the screen, but the Soda there had vanished.

* * *

ARI CAME TO AND BLINKED, looking around her and wondering what had happened. The last thing she remembered was the bright light. Her face hurt, but she didn't feel any wet blood or obvious injuries other than the spot on her shoulder where Lrrrje had nicked her with the Stingr. The camera was nearby on the ground. The TPHWs were gone. So was Soda.

Nearby, Kirian moaned and rolled onto her stomach. Ari could hear her still breathing in ragged gasps.

Ari scrambled to her feet and rushed to help her.

At exactly that moment the song ended. The reverb hung around a few extra seconds in the atmosphere and then died away.

"Ari," Kirian said, "you did it."

Kirian held her hands up to Ari. Her handcuffs were gone.

Ari stood in stunned silence. She hadn't expected that.

She ran over to Kirian. "Let's get back to the ship before anything else happens," Ari said.

She helped Kirian stand and pulled out her communicator. "Fleek, can you come and pick us up? Kracken stole our portal, remember? Oh, and Fleek?"

"Yes?"

"Loved the song."

Chapter 27

While Trisha looked on, probably in shock, the Octopus and the dogs disappeared, and the song ended.

Her phone chimed. She checked it. Her message had eventually gone through, and Jen finally replied.

Your favorite sandwich place closed. Frowny face emoji.

Trisha looked up at Brad. "Communications have been restored! What do you think it means?"

He shook his head. A space ship entered orbit and picked up the warrior girl and the tourist with the television camera who'd been hit by the meteor.

The only thing left of the downtown melee was a few plumes of smoke and four or five blocks worth of destruction.

People were coming out of buildings tentatively, looking around and taking pictures. Trisha scanned nervously for signs of a giant, bloodied Preying Mantis with a briefcase and an arm sticking out of its mouth, but she saw nothing unusual. No dogs, no Overseer, no Mantis.

Then it hit her. She was done. She could go back and finish her thesis. And then she could sleep. Of course, nobody would believe her. But it didn't matter; she had enough photos to include in the document and plenty of points to finish.

Ten minutes later, as Trisha and Brad were waiting to go through the portal to get back to their lives, Regulus issued an Official Planetary Statement in conjunction with the Neon Octopus Overseer:

THE UNUSUAL EVENTS and damage to the planet of Regulus were the result of a gas leak. The resultant explosion caused mass hallucinatory effects throughout the whole downtown area. Any giant dogs, octopi that may or may not resemble the Overseer herself, mythical female warriors, Preying Mantises, experimental camera guns, or meteors that may or may not have been seen were purely imaginary. Except for the illegal, pirated, kick-ass rock concert. That part was real. You're welcome.

* * *

FLOYD RE-ENTERED THE SHIP. The wide-eyed captain had maximum warp keyed into the controls.

"Do you see the crazy communications coming in from Regulus?" he asked. "Are you okay?"

"I know," Floyd answered excitedly. "Everything down there was a huge scandal. I can't wait for a full and thorough investigation of the whole thing."

Within seconds, they were safely on their way back to Arcturis City. He smiled. The plan had worked, communications were coming in, and Soda was screwed.

Then the Official Planetary Statement in conjunction with the Neon Octopus Overseer notification buzzed onto his phone.

"Son of a star!" he screamed.

* * *

FLEEK SCOOPED up the girls with his tracking beam. Once onboard, Ari covered her eyes to shield them from the extra light.

"What in stars happened here?" she asked. "I can barely see."

"Marco, the guitarist, fixed the power problem," Fleek said.

"What power problem?" Ari asked. Not that it mattered. Not much of anything mattered. She noticed Fleek was still staring at her.

"What happened to your face?" he asked her.

"What happened to your face?" she retorted. Then realized he was distracting her from figuring out what had happened on the planet.

She ran to the console and brought up an image of Regulus. There was plenty of smoke and damage, but there were no longer any TPHWs, no crazy Preying Mantis, and no Neon Octopus Overlord. People were coming out of hiding. "How do you like that?" she said. "It looks like the planet's going to be okay."

Ari checked communications next. It had been fully restored. Messages were flowing off of the planet and around the galaxy again. She wondered what Soda was going to think of that. It probably wasn't going to be pretty.

Then she received the statement put out by the Official Planetary Authorities and made in conjunction with the Neon Octopus Overlord.

She read it. Twice.

"You gotta be kidding me," she said, attracting the attention of the others. "Soda's claiming the whole thing was a mass hallucination."

She and Kirian embraced. Kirian and Fleek embraced. Bloody and wounded, Kirian wouldn't stop smiling. She showed everybody that her bracelet restraints were gone.

Ari even hugged the new band member she didn't know. There were happy shouts and whoops. Fleek changed the console back to incoming communication, and fan messages praising the song scrolled in by the thousands.

"Listen, everybody," Fleek said, "I sent portal invites to all of the biggest rock stars! Every one of them accepted our invitation to join us on my ship. This is going to be the biggest party the galaxy has ever seen. Invite your friends."

"Somebody invite a doctor, too," Ari said, looking at Kirian.

They partied well into the night. A doctor, happy to be invited, treated Kirian's wounds.

Fleek jumped on a chair to raise a toast. "To Chemical Zombies!" A cheer erupted. "To Kirian, Destroyer of Planets!" Kirian took a bow. "And to Ari, the galaxy's most wanted."

Ari smiled. She didn't care that she was wanted. Not tonight. Tonight, she was Ari, space traveler and Defender of Worlds.

She was traveling the galaxy with an ex-Celestial and a newly-famous rock band, and she loved every minute of it.

After the party ended, she was left with a feeling of peace, and a view of the stars from her bedroom window.

* * *

DREXYL STARED at the screen in shock. Kirian was free. The drones took close-up views of Kirian's naked wrists. Kirian and Ari were scooped up by a space ship and then they disappeared.

Soda broke into long, melodious laughter. It came in waves, undulating for minutes.

"What's so funny?" Drexyl asked.

"They think they won," Soda said.

"They did. I mean, didn't they?"

"Oh, Kirian may be free of me for now, that much may be true. But with the footage I've been collecting from Celestial, I'll make her the most wanted being in this galaxy. TPHWs will be nothing compared to what's coming for her. By the time she figures out how high a price I've placed on her head, it will already be on a plate." She turned to Drexyl. "I play all the angles, my dear, and I don't play to lose."

ABOUT THE AUTHOR

L.A. Johnson writes fun, original Sci-Fi you won't find anywhere else.

Available for Pre-Order
Whisperer to Stars:
Book Two of the Neon Octopus Overlord Series

Pre-Order Whisperer to Stars on Amazon

Connect with me
www.lajbooks.com

ACKNOWLEDGMENTS

First of all, I'd like to thank my husband, Kerry for his ceaseless encouragement, support, and feedback.

I'd like to thank my Mom and Dad for always believing in me and always being there for me.

To my friend Alex who has shared the writers' journey with me and all of its ups and downs.

And then there's Nathan Lowell who is not only a brilliant storyteller but a wonderful mentor as well. Thank you.

I'd also like to give a shout out to PixelmatorNinja for their blog doodle that reminded me of Soda.

And of course, I give all thanks to God, from whom all peace and blessings flow.

Made in the USA
Middletown, DE
22 September 2018